Chapter One

Another day; a new week. Driving to work at the large Business Machines, Incorporated facility north of Denver, Colorado, as he has for three years, Greg turns west as the late spring sun is just now ascending behind him. He watches its gracious light illuminate the Front Range ahead. The effect causes several windows of distant, settled houses on purple slopes beyond to sparkle magically, making temporary stars of them as would guide ancient mariners upon the sea.

Opportunities are like that. Moments of glittering intensity can appear here and there and something grand results at that fortunate conjunction. Passing time, however, may soon reduce the momentum, and a fortuitous intersection will be lost if one is incautious. Other chances may certainly arise later, but the one is gone for good. A person must accept that before he can move on.

Fifteen years earlier, Greg was at the height of his professional life. A select instructor at the United States Air Force Academy in Colorado Springs, each move programmed for continued greatness, his career had literally taken off. His personal life, however, withered in that rarefied air. He had reached a stage where he wished for more, to soar higher still until he grasped the one quality that his life then lacked: love.

Icarus may now be but a venerable myth, a tired cliché even, yet the new wings that Greg was proudly donning for the first time at the Academy were untried. He temporarily forgot that every object aloft must eventually settle back to earth. Since airborne formations are a conspicuous target, he was more vulnerable than he imagined. One can either make preparations for a soft landing, or rise as if indestructible and inevitably crash.

In his rapid descent, he lost nearly everything he had once valued, everything he had become.

It didn't matter that betrayal played the greater part in this personal tragedy. Still, Fate usually provides some sort of cushion if one is determined to rebound. (Any landing one can walk away from is deemed a success.) Greg was nothing if not resilient, knowing that time is of variable duration for those who are patient enough to wait it out. And lofty eminence may yet come again.

Given the circumstances, his military career terminated, his emergency funds nearly spent, he finally got a job and eventually recovered. Wary but undaunted, he now carefully takes the new turns that life currently guides him through. As the years progress, he becomes less concerned with what lies on the road ahead and more preoccupied with how he might master any new success, this time without being blindsided. He consults the rear and side mirrors more frequently, caution replacing his formerly heady naiveté. Occasionally, he trusts others and is usually disappointed once again. But he never allows the stakes to become as high as they once had been. Never again does he position himself to lose everything for someone else. Potential love is no longer worth the ultimate gamble even though the love of someone whom he loves is as important to him as ever.

Greg knows as much as anyone that love is who you are. A career merely defines the intervals.

Chapter Two

Parking his car at the far end of one of the large BMI parking lots that surround the extensive facility, Greg crosses a vast expanse of blacktop to reach the nearest of several turnstiles, intermittently placed, and badges himself through. He walks several more steps to the building where he works and badges himself in at the door.

"I really think they're employing overkill," he muses to himself, reflecting upon the latest policy requiring the use of one's ID badge to gain admittance to every building on site, even if one has already obtained entrance to the complex through the outer perimeter fence.

He walks past several hallways and corridors to his own office. Closing the door, he turns on the switch of his network computer and watches the screen come alive. Typing three different passwords on three different screens allows him to begin work.

He prefers coming in earlier than most of the others on this team. These several minutes of peaceful quiet are important to him before his co-workers arrive and the day becomes more hectic.

This isn't a bad assignment for a contract technical writer, reviewing and revising the various online BMI sales manual hardware and software documents that arrive over a vast, worldwide network to the small group that he works with. Only the project manager and the team leader are actually BMI employees; the rest are, like himself, contractors, assigned for the length of the project, without benefits of any kind. The latest form of migrant worker, anyone can be terminated anytime without reason given or notice provided; but at least the pay is good. Ultimately, a better salary is what induced Greg to leave Colorado Springs for this overly officious occupation. That, and the fact that he wasn't able to find any other full-time work in Colorado Springs after his last full-time job ended there.

A door closes; another opens. Eventually. Like some great maze set off in various directions, with eventual passages as yet unclear, he negotiates the most direct path before him.

Actually, it wasn't as if he'd ever had much of a choice at each of the several abrupt turns in his own life. Ever since leaving the Academy, whenever several possibilities seemed to appear, only one actually played out; and he did have to spend several unemployed intervals before the next door opened, revealing that an apparent dead end had a sole and fortuitous opening after all.

Greg occasionally wonders if he might ever have the opportunity to lift himself up above his current existence and look at the entire span of his life. Would he, in fact, be viewing a complex maze, one with several, built-in possibilities that he'd never noticed or allowed himself to consider? Or would he see but a single path possible, circuitous perhaps, but puzzling only in its direct simplicity, like some grand connect-the-dots drawing? And what kind of picture would his life's efforts reveal when all of the dots are conjoined?

Right now, however, to him the image seems incomplete, unfulfilled. Several dots must still be out there, lying unconnected, he believes, waiting for him to find the junction.

A year earlier, when his previous BMI contract assignment ended, a bizarre prospect arose. The Air Force Academy was mandated to hire several civilian instructors to augment their entirely military faculty. Greg thought that Fate was perversely turning his life back, allowing him to reconnect, after a 14-year absence, at the very point where he felt his existence had become disjointed.

During the 12 years when he still lived in the Springs, he had taught part-time college courses at the other two military bases, expanding and perfecting his teaching skills. His full-time jobs had involved technical writing and an intense use of computers, both qualifications demanded at this new Academy assignment. He felt that coincidence was operating in his favor this time, making him the ideal candidate; so he applied, expecting that he'd be selected. He was so certain that an old wrong would now, finally, be righted.

He was mistaken. Apparently, his life moves always forward, with no backtracking. Of the more than 100 applicants, the English Department conveniently hired someone else.

Life is rarely like literature, Greg determined, even when it has seemed to be fated. He returned to the minutia of his everyday existence, this latest BMI assignment came through, and he wondered

4

if he had been entirely wrong all along about his having a life charmed by circumstance.

Andy Warhol had certainly exaggerated; not everyone gets 15 minutes. The vast majority of humanity pass through history virtually unnoticed, except in their sheer numbers, their obvious bulk. Especially in the modern era, people are lucky if they aren't entirely overlooked in a census, appear on infrequent voter roles, rate an audit by the IRS, or get a modest obituary at their passing. Most are simply neglected, like emaciated peasants in a foreign land, working stubborn and furrowed fields, perpetually hungry, yet insufficiently fortunate to be touched by a newsworthy famine, one severe enough to obtain outside relief.

On his now-familiar route returning from work, even though he is traveling in the opposite direction from most of the other drivers, Greg notes that traffic levels both ways have increased over the previous three years, particularly most recently. He has only to look around to see some of the reasons: a new library is being built downtown, a new amusement park is going up near the Interstate, the new and much-maligned airport is nearing completion out on the plains to the east of the city, and all around Denver, new bridges, overpasses, and more lanes in an expanding freeway system are appearing. Old viaducts, some constructed nearly a century ago with the supreme efforts of hardy workers long gone, are coming down. Here, unlike elsewhere in the nation, are jobs.

"Hey, look out, asshole," Greg shouts at the other driver who is cutting him off. When Greg sounds a warning horn, the other guy flips him off.

"I get tired of being given the finger when the other guy is in the wrong," Greg laments.

With more cars comes less civility, everywhere, it seems. Greg looks around at other drivers nearby. Each has retreated into his or her own personal world. The guy ahead is talking animatedly on his cellular phone. The woman to Greg's right appears to be delving into a purse on the seat beside her. The guy on his left is taking a long and distracted drag on a cigarette, blowing smoke out the sunroof. The couple in the car behind is having a face-to-face

5

conversation. None of their obvious negligence would seem so scary were they not all going well over 65 mph in a 55 mph zone.

Greg sighs and then also retreats, pushing the automatic controls to close his windows, switching on the air conditioning, and turning up the volume of his car CD player, trying his best to tune out an increasingly rude and confusing world.

From a few friends whom he left behind in Colorado Springs, he is told that traffic levels and trouble are not much different there, what with so many conservative religious groups moving their headquarters to that city. With fires, earthquakes, celebrity murders, and public riots in California where he grew up, and where some family members and friends still live, he knows of no good reason to return there. Besides, many Californians, as well as Texans, are moving to Colorado, hoping for a better life, or a job at least.

No, Denver isn't as bad as other places seem to be. He will stay, for now, and make the best of it, he reasons.

At the 38th Street exit, Greg hits his turn signal and changes lanes and is surprised that someone else hasn't pulled ahead to cut off his attempt to exit the freeway. He eases up to the stoplight and is also surprised not to see one of the many men or women who stand outdoors in all weather with a creased and faded cardboard sign, asking for money: "Hungry. Will work for food. God bless you."

At least this day Greg will not feel guilty driving by and leaving nothing. However, a friend told him recently, "It's a scam! They all work for some guy who pays them a commission for what they collect. If you offered them a job, they wouldn't take it."

Greg isn't so convinced. Some of them certainly *look* extremely needy.

When the light changes, he turns left under the freeway overpass, and then heads up the shiny new viaduct that edges Denver's new baseball stadium, Coors Field, still under construction but set to open next spring.

"Jeeze," Greg exclaims, noticing that youthful taggers have already left their urban scrawl on a just completed, concrete abutment. The large, dark, incomprehensible lettering beams annoyingly in the bright sunlight, deepening his mood.

6

"This bridge isn't even a week old, and they've already gotten to it," he laments, finding it increasingly difficult not to yield to cynicism.

Chapter Three

After a vigorous workout at the new athletic facility on Colorado Boulevard, Greg heads to his apartment near Cheesman Park. The park itself, before the end of the 19th century, had been a cemetery. As in the movie *Poltergeist*, all of the tombstones were removed long ago, but not so all of the bodies. Over a thousand were left unclaimed and, presumably, undisturbed, although no one now seems to know exactly where those mortal remains currently rest. Some could as easily reside under the very grass and soil where Greg and several of his acquaintances engage in volleyball matches on summer afternoons. Not that this macabre possibility disturbs their play.

Humboldt Street, the first block west of Cheesman Park, where Greg's apartment complex is located, is one of several, tree-lined, historic districts in the Capitol Hill region of Denver, known simply as "The Hill" by locals.

Several majestic and expensive mansions quaintly line two of the blocks to the north. Directly across the street from his early 1970's-era building is a high-rise of even newer vintage, two condos to a floor, fifteen stories high. It towers on the site where rumor places the old mansion described in grim detail in the novel *The Omen*. On a dark, forbidding fall evening, when the moon is full and leaves panic at the mere touch of an autumn wind, one might feel the grip of morbid death all about. But, no. This is a rather quiet and sedate urban neighborhood in any season of the year. No moans awaken the night, except for an occasional, illicit sexual encounter in the bushes along the edge of the park. The only rattling that one hears is from the pilfered shopping carts pushed down the alley behind his building in the early morning hours by street people who frequent the dumpsters for discarded treasure.

The Molly Brown house is a few blocks away to the northwest. The well-known "Queen" Soopers grocery store is due west, four blocks, catty-corner to a liquor store and a hardware store, further west. A card shop, video store, ice cream parlor, barbershop, tailor, and sandwich shop all nestle together in one building a block east of the supermarket, along 9th Street. A large, recently refurbished elementary school stands across 9th from the supermarket. In many ways, this area reflects Main Street, USA.

All of the distinct amenities of suburban living are provided in an urban setting, within easy walking distance, and just a few miles from downtown Denver.

Greg's apartment on the second floor overlooks 10th Street that runs east/west, stopping at the edge of the Park. His two cats, Sneezer and Schnozz, are always at the door to greet him. (They are expecting to be fed.) Sneezer, left behind two years earlier by a former live-in boyfriend, is a large and often lethargic, six-year-old, neutered silver tabby. Schnozz, who was raised from a kitten in Greg's house in Colorado Springs, is approximately 13 years old. A longhaired, multicolored, finicky but beautiful, spayed female with Siamese bone structure, Schnozz makes her presence felt at all times subtly. If she doesn't get what she wants, or feels that she has had quite enough play for the time being, she nips. Not enough to break skin although she used to draw blood in her wild youth. She also used to scratch. But that was a long time ago.

Now, mellowed into passive-aggressiveness, she pees or poops surreptitiously outside her litter box to show infrequent displeasure at being fed too late or having to share affection with Sneezer, whom she openly despises. Usually, she starts their tussles; however, Sneezer is both bigger and heavier and wins eventually by pinning her to the carpet and licking her face. She hates this effrontery and tries to nip an ear when he isn't looking. Greg referees.

Chapter Four

Greg uses his evenings, as most others do, to recover from the day. Evenings, however, like weekends, seem to have diminished in duration almost incessantly as he's gotten older. Even more so since the early '80's. This all seemed to start during the Reagan Administration and has only gotten worse in the many years since.

He turns on *Headline News*, an occasionally ghoulish backdrop to preparing dinner, given the bloody state of the world lately. Schnozz shamelessly hangs around the kitchen even after she's been fed on the premise that something in a skillet or on a plate will find its way to the floor, her domain. Gravity is, after all, the natural ally of creatures built closer to the ground.

Besides, Greg has indulged and even spoiled her for years. Sneezer, on the other hand, made more compliant by his previous owners, who had inexplicably deposited him at the Denver Dumb Friends League two years ago, declawed, does not abide human food. He usually tries to bury it.

On the television this night is yet another of the sly commercials financed by the Religious Right, coolly extolling the virtues of procreation and claiming an endless availability of chairs at life's dinner table.

"Yeah, right," Greg exclaims in response, leaning into the living room from the kitchen. "Try rush hour traffic and see if you still want infinitely more humans to contend with!"

Raised for all the years of his youth as a Catholic, he now has little toleration for organized religions of any persuasion, given the amount of suffering he sees on the TV each night and in the newspaper each morning. On an infrequent visit to the Springs to see how his tenants are caring for the house he still owns there, he has noticed more and more impressive church structures going up, most of them in an odd competition with one another over a finite number of souls and the same, infinite God. Churches and temples and synagogues stand empty much of the day and night while the number of homeless people living on the streets and under bridges increases.

Simultaneously, especially in states like Colorado, which are becoming less and less rural as humans move farther afield, he sees an increasing clash between animals and Homo sapiens. Greg is beginning to harbor more sympathy for the animals, shunted aside today, much as the first human inhabitants of America were herded onto reservations years ago by European immigrants. After all, he reasons, lions and tigers and bears do not drive the freeways unmercifully.

He was not at all surprised when he heard that in the aftermath of a California mountain lion attack upon a woman jogger--fatal ultimately for both creatures--that the lion's orphaned cub was initially receiving a greater outpouring of donations than the orphaned human children. Obviously, he isn't the only one who feels like easing away just a bit from unqualified and total support for his own species at the expense of everything else.

Chapter Five

Thumbing through the TV schedule for something to watch during dinner, this night on Denver's Public Television station Greg notices that one of his favorite speakers will debut his newest lecture: *Homophobia in the Workplace.* Suspicious, however, since Channel 12 virtually never airs gay-themed programming this early in the evening unless they are using the opportunity to entice gay and lesbian viewers to support their quarterly fund-raiser, Greg switches on the set.

"I knew it," he laughs, sitting down on the couch to savor this PBS station's blatant manipulation of its gay audience for revenue.

The familiar face of Denver gay radio personality Mason Lewis appears on the screen, fronting two banks of phone volunteers.

"In order to present programming of this kind," Lewis admonishes, "we need support from viewers like you. If we don't have the funding, Channel 12 won't be able to air programs like *Homophobia in the Workplace* which was recorded right here in Channel 12's own studio."

Mason then announces, "In fact, up to this point in the evening, we're getting more hate calls than pledge calls."

Knowing that he is likely being manipulated still further, the mention of antigay hate calls always gets Greg's blood heated, so he reaches for the phone to make his usual contribution.

Lewis continues exhorting the viewers: "You can pledge $25, $75, or $125 and charge it to your MasterCard or Visa. Answering phones for us this evening are members of the Rainbow Arc of Fire, a gay pagan group."

Greg perks up at this interesting revelation and stops dialing.

Lewis has moved over to the lower phone bank, directing his conversation to one of the volunteers: "Joseph Johnson is a spokesman for the group. Tell us, Joseph, a little about the Rainbow Arc of Fire."

Joseph cheerfully explains, "We are a pagan group that believes in the spirituality of the Earth and the power of elemental

12

forces. We are just one chapter out of many that have sprung up all over the country. Since most organized religions have rejected gay members, we feel that we fulfill an important need in the gay community by providing an alternative form of worship that abandons any sense of personal guilt."

"How large is your membership?"

"Quite large, actually," Joseph continues. "Our chapter is growing monthly. People appreciate the spiritual message that we provide because we don't claim to have *the* answer. We simply offer one method of reexamining one's ties to the Earth, ties that we feel have been lost in the modern world."

"How can someone learn more about your group?"

"Our phone number is listed with the Gay and Lesbian Community Center of Colorado. Anyone who wishes to attend our monthly meetings, or participate in one of our seasonal encampments, is encouraged to contact us through the GLCCC."

"That's wonderful," Mason concludes, turning again to the camera. "The Rainbow Arc of Fire is just one of several gay organizations here tonight that have volunteered their time to take your telephone pledges. Please call in now and pledge whatever you can so that Channel 12 can continue to support all facets of the gay community in Denver through its diverse programming."

Greg finishes dialing, makes his usual contribution, and hangs up, intrigued with this new organization he's not heard about before. He is barely able to focus on Brian McNaught's fascinating lecture. Fortunately, pledging at the level he did, Greg was assured that he will be sent a videotape of the program.

As usual, at 9:00 PM, Greg shuts off the TV with the remote and announces, "Time to go to bed, kitties."

Sneezer remains on the couch, his usual nocturnal habitat, yawns, and lays his fuzzy chin back down on the firm cushion.

As Greg turns out the last light, Schnozz hops to the floor and precedes him down the long hall to the back bedroom, her fluffy puff of a tail dancing ahead in the semi-dark. In the bedroom she jumps from the floor to the bed, and thence to her carpeted cat perch, a tall cylinder placed against the window ledge where she can watch any curious cars on the street or people passing by on the sidewalk below.

In the early morning hours, either she or Sneezer will be found curled up or sitting attentively on the end of the bed, waiting for their owner to get up and feed them before he again goes off to work.

Greg takes a pillow from the closet shelf, safe during the day from an unpredictably vengeful feline, tosses it to the head of the bed, and climbs under a single sheet for warmth since late spring has been rather hot this year. He falls asleep quite easily to the sound of the box fan set on low in the window, humming almost noiselessly.

The night is unusually still. No distant sirens scream, no nearby cars race noisily down the street, to disturb this unique tranquillity. A low whistle of a freight train pulling into the yards a few miles away is smothered by the "white noise" of the fan. It is as if the entire city, this night, has decided to sleep the sleep of complete innocence, as if for the first time.

Well after midnight, Greg begins to dream in earnest. He is in a clearing, deep in a wooded glen. The trees are in their darker rustlings, as mountain pines are wont to do when the wind eases heavily amongst their dense numbers. Arranged about the edge of the forest are small tents, ringing a central fire. Several men, half naked, can be seen cavorting about the enclosed flames, circumscribed by solid stones, arrayed geometrically. Hands clasped in union, their faces are painted many colors; but the rainbow shades assume the shape of a sacred arc across their foreheads.

All are smiling in revelry as rainbows, continuously forming like tongues from the flames, lick their bronzed bodies. Communal chanting begins, ever so softly at first, as if each voice is too new at this, and even a bit shy, to partake of such a singular pleasure so fully.

But then, emboldened by so many numbers like themselves, they increase their benediction until the very clouds above are touched. Next, a slow and consecrating rain cascades over them, washing the scenery clean, except for the men, who smear their chests with primal mud and continue dancing. As the minutes of ecstasy pass and profound weariness overtakes them, first two, and then a few others, pair off, retiring to the various tents at the first sight of morning light through the foliage.

14

Greg, one with them now, watches the pairs move away from the sizzling charcoals, now almost entirely spent.

He picks up one charred and forked stake of wood and brings it near his nostrils to inhale of its depleted essence. It smells instead like a dampened forest, renewed, and this revelation startles him. He opens his eyes slowly to see the wide, furry face of Schnozz, backing away, having touched her nose to his and awakened him. He glances at the digital clock, its red numbers glowing pointedly. It's still too early to get up.

"Go back to sleep, Schnozz," Greg mumbles., rolling over.

Although he, too, curls up again in fetal contentment and dozes off, he still remembers the vivid dream of a place he is certain he has never been to before, a place that at once felt so familiar.

15

Chapter Six

Intending to call the GLCCC for the pagan group's phone number, the week has gotten away from him and the day is Friday. Instead, after working at BMI and making a brief stop at the apartment to check the mail and phone machine and feed the cats, Greg heads to *Garbo's*, a smallish piano bar on 9th Street, between Lincoln and Sherman Streets, known for its Friday after-work crowd.

Paying for his usual Black Current Calistoga and tipping his favorite bartender, the only woman on the staff, he retreats to his typical spot by the entrance, next to the large, white grand piano. From this vantage point, he can watch everyone arriving and departing for the next couple of hours.

He realizes that he has become a fixture most Friday nights simply because there are few other establishments now that cater to someone over 40 since *Buddies*, a once-popular dance bar, closed two years earlier. *Charlie's* is a popular Country and Western bar, and he occasionally dons his cowboy boots and Bailey's Clint Black cowboy hat, ambling over there on a Saturday night, although he only likes selected country songs and doesn't know any of the dances. *The Triangle* is a darkened leather bar, and he usually avoids it. The several other bars in Denver only seem to attract those who are 21 to 35, or those who are looking only for someone 21 to 35. He quickly tires of feeling like a chaperone, so he doesn't go anywhere else.

Some friends encourage him to try the personals; however, reading them each month depresses him. Most of those men who advertise themselves, no matter their age, are looking for someone younger, often someone much younger: "Wealthy 45-year-old Greek God looking for compliant 25-year-old Adonis for Long Term Relationship, or one-night stand. Serious replies only. No fats, fems, or druggies."

On the other side of the spectrum, their requirements seem equally demanding: "You must be rich, well-endowed, handsome, have a cabin in the mountains and condo in the city, drive an expensive Mercedes--will accept new BMW sedan--and be willing to endure my excessive demands and widely divergent mood swings. Send recent photo and copies of IRS tax returns for the previous five years. I'm young, beautiful, restless, and worth it." Signed, "Sincere."

Never one to trust anyone "sight unseen," Greg muddles along with those he meets in the bars, at the gym, or playing volleyball in the Park. After more than three years in Denver, the choices have become quite slim, discounting those who have already deemed themselves disinterested.

Some people have told him, "You won't meet anyone if you're looking." Which seems to Greg the equivalent of saying that you won't win the state lottery by playing. As if the right person is simply going to drop out of the sky and fall into his lap, almost by accident.

It's still early at Garbo's. Most of the crowd will begin to arrive after 6:30 PM, Greg knows. A few are here early, as usual, particularly those who sit at the bar, smoking, drinking, and conversing amongst themselves. Standing a few feet from the bar saves him from the worst of the smoke, and his eyes wander to the tables and booths at this level, and then on to those on the lower level, toward the back.

More than a year ago, the owner invested in a lot of red. (Maybe there was a sale.) That would be fine for the Christmas season, or even for Valentine's Day; but since nearly every square foot of wall space is mirrored from ceiling to floor, the effect of an apparently endless number of bright red chairs, tables, and booths, heading off into infinity, is overwhelming, as well as tacky. The place looks more like a Through-the-Looking-Glass bordello. Fortunately, although the bar itself was also covered in radiant red, and even the deep green carpet has red dots, the piano, mercifully, was left white.

Now that his eyes have adjusted to the semidarkness and the countless reflections in each direction, Greg notices a small group of unfamiliar men in a booth on the lower level, talking animatedly. One of their number, however, looks quite familiar, and Greg cannot figure out why. Suddenly, he recalls the Channel 12 fund-raiser. The

17

brown-haired man who looks to be in his middle 30's is the telephone volunteer from the pagan group.

What is his name? Jonathan? No, Joseph.

Greg finds himself staring now, for the other is certainly not unattractive. However, the way that the guy next to Joseph is sitting closely, Greg assumes that the two are lovers. "The good ones are *always* taken," he sighs, taking another sip from the Calistoga.

More importantly, though, he'd rather like to meet them, to find out why they have become pagans and what forms their rituals take.

While stationed in North Dakota with the Air Force before moving to Colorado, Greg recalls that he once knew a graduate of the Academy also assigned there who was a devout atheist, who sent out Winter Solstice cards at Christmas instead of Christmas cards; but he has never before met a pagan.

At this moment, Joseph is getting up from the table. He ascends the steps to the main level and is heading toward the short hallway and the rest rooms beyond. He notices that he is being observed, so he turns and smiles at Greg and waves. Greg returns the gracious smile and the wave.

"He seems friendly," Greg acknowledges to himself, surprised. However, smiling and greeting someone across the room is not the same as meeting him, and Greg suddenly can't think of a single way to enhance that first contact.

Joseph, soon returning from the rest room, has turned toward Greg and is approaching, smiling again, hand outstretched, "Hello, my name is Joseph. Have we met?"

"I'm sorry," Greg confesses, wishing that he could be that self-confident while shaking Joseph's proffered hand. "We haven't met."

Still, he muddles onward, "My name's Greg. I saw you the other night on Channel 12's fund-raiser. I was intrigued that you are a pagan. I've never met a pagan before."

Joseph knowingly chuckles, having heard this sort of remark many times, "Well, now you have. Would you like to join us? We're having an informal meeting about our encampment this weekend in the mountains."

18

"Really?" Greg replies, intrigued by this revelation while attempting to overcome most of his own inherent shyness at meeting total strangers, even in a small group.

"Yes," Joseph confirms, hoping that he has sparked additional interest in their group, interest that might yield to something further. "Sunday is the Summer Solstice, you know. We like to be up in the mountains for our ceremonies as the sun comes up."

"I didn't know that," Greg admits, intrigued enough to find out more. "I certainly would like to join your meeting, if you don't mind."

"Not at all," Joseph sincerely replies as he leads the way back down the stairs to the lower level and the table of other pagans.

"Everyone," he soon announces, a comforting hand on Greg's shoulder, "This is Greg. He's never met any pagans before, at least none that he *knows* were pagans; and so I thought he might like to join us."

"That's great," one of them says. "We need a volunteer to be our human sacrifice this weekend."

Everyone smiles conspiratorially and nods, and then they look at one another and laugh at the obvious joke. Joseph interrupts them and turns to Greg, "He's only kidding. The one with the warped sense of humor is my lover, William."

William nods, smiling, "Pleased to meet you."

"Next to William is Henry. Then Richard, Henry's lover. And finally, Geoffrey, whose lover James is out of town this weekend."

"Hi," Greg nods, realizing that he hasn't actually caught all of their names the first time around, though he did catch the fact that all of them are in relationships.

"Here," Geoffrey offers, a strikingly handsome man in his early 40's, who scoots over and pulls up a chair for Greg to join them. "Have a seat."

"Thanks."

Greg nervously sits down but forces himself to look around the table at the varied group, who seem to range in age from their late 20's to early 50's. However, he's totally unsure of what to say next.

19

Joseph eases the momentary silence by adding, "I told Greg about our Summer Solstice celebration this weekend."

"Uh, oh," William warns, devilishly grinning again, "he'll have to join us now or we'll be *forced* to sacrifice him."

Joseph eyes his lover narrowly, knowing how some strangers often do not know how to respond to this kind of teasing, "That's enough, William. Christians have given us such a bad reputation over the past 1000 years and more; your jokes are *not* helping."

"Oh," Greg smiles and assures them, "I'm not a Christian."

"Another potential recruit, then?" Henry interjects, chuckling, a short, stocky man in his early 50's, with a lively face and thinning gray hair.

"Maybe," Greg admits, committing himself no further, for now.

"Do you have any plans this weekend?" Joseph pointedly asks, hoping that Greg will join them, sensing that his interest in their group appears genuine.

"Not really," Greg confesses, now warming a bit more to the idea of meeting new people in unfamiliar surroundings. "When are you going up into the mountains?"

"We usually drive up on Saturday morning if the Solstice is on Sunday," Geoffrey explains. "Then, we return to the city on Sunday evening. Most of us have to work Monday morning."

"So do I," Greg tells them. "Unfortunately, though, I don't have a tent or a sleeping bag."

"That's all right," Geoffrey interjects. "My boyfriend James isn't coming with us since he's back East on a business trip, so you can bunk in our tent. We've got an extra sleeping bag, too."

"Then it's settled," Joseph nods, obviously pleased. "You can give Geoffrey your phone number and address, and he can swing by and pick you up tomorrow morning."

Greg then borrows a pen from their waiter and writes his name, phone number, and address on a matchbook and hands it to Geoffrey.

"May I bring anything?" he asks, unsure of what their rituals require.

"You mean other than 'Eye of Newt and Wing of Bat?'" William teases, knowing that, in the minds of some, pagan rituals are frequently confused with those of practicing witches.

"You need not bring anything, really," Joseph sighs, shaking his head at William. "Geoffrey will be stopping by the market to pick up bottled water, so you can help him with that tomorrow morning."

Geoffrey does add, "Just bring some warm clothing. Hiking boots and flannel shirts, if you've got them. Shorts are fine during the day, but you might want to have Levis for the evening and early morning in case the weather turns cold. This time of year, there's no telling."

Greg nods, grateful for the sound advice. He thinks it best not to mention the dream he had the other night of the half-naked bodies, dancing in the dark. He isn't sure if the others will feel insulted by his dream of libidinous ecstasy.

Their meeting soon concludes. As they leave *Garbo's*, stepping out the front door as the pale purple of evening eases over the city, Greg sincerely remarks, "It was certainly quite a coincidence that I met all of you here this night after having seen you on TV just a few days ago."

"Oh?" Joseph replies, suddenly becoming serious. "Actually, we don't believe in coincidence."

Chapter Seven

Even though this is Saturday morning, and Geoffrey had called later on Friday evening to say that he would be by at 7:00 AM to pick him up, Greg cannot sleep past 5:00. Sneezer won't let him. The big guy is already roaming back and forth across the bed when he senses—probably by the clock in his stomach—that the usual time has arrived for his owner to get up during the week.

Cats obviously don't understand the concept of a weekend because, for them, every day of the week they're off. They don't have to go to work. This day neither does Greg, but his admonition to Sneezer to "Sit!" only lasts momentarily. Sneezer plops his rump down on the bed like a canine would obey his master; but soon he stretches himself, stands up, and begins pacing again. Schnozz sits nearby, expectantly.

"OK, guys, OK," sighs Greg, yawning. "I'm up. I'll feed you."

He wearily makes his way down the hall with half-opened eyes, then shuffles past the living room, and finally turns into the tiny kitchen. Opening the door of the refrigerator, the bright light nearly stunning him, he spies two of the small margarine tubs he reuses for storing moist cat food after opening a large can the day before, divvying up the contents into eight separate portions, four meals per cat. Sneezer and Schnozz are weaving between his legs, jockeying for position at their bowls as he empties the contents of the two tubs.

His friend Ramsey has promised to feed the two beasts on Saturday evening and Sunday morning while Greg is away with the pagans. Although Sneezer wouldn't miss his moist meal as much since he also eats plenty of dry cat food from the feeder, Schnozz would probably seek revenge for having a primary need ignored, even once. Greg dares not risk her feline, feminine wrath.

On his way back to bed, he pauses at the front door and opens it. Schnozz likes to wander out onto the landing, which looks down on the courtyard and fountain below, then climb up two flights of stairs, and spend a few minutes alone on the sun deck, on the roof above the third floor apartments, apparently watching and listening as the city awakens all around her. He usually finds her sitting up there, ears poised intently for the sound of birds flying by or dogs barking in the distance, or for something even humans cannot see or hear.

This behavior seems primal because she used to do that at their home in Colorado Springs where she had a big expanse of back lawn to traverse and neighbors' fences to climb upon and sit atop, surveying her spacious domain. Her adjustment to an apartment in the city, and another cat in residence, has probably been difficult, although she is not able to verbally express herself. Greg wonders if she still remembers the home where she grew up and spent 11 years of her life, or if that entire existence has faded back into the mists of her memory, like legend or myth.

Why he hangs onto his house in the Springs after the Amendment 2 controversy is probably why he still tries to maintain his '73 Camaro in the parking lot downstairs, the first new car he ever owned; in addition to the first and only home he's ever owned. It's the same reason that he keeps Schnozz, despite her several quirks. He cannot let go of some things from the past because they still have meaning for him.

Others would certainly not tolerate her aberrant behavior, her moodiness and jealousies. Frank, the ex-boyfriend, even tried to kill her once when she scratched him. He had terrorized her before, and Greg, too. Both were afraid of his violent mood swings. After the drunken night when Frank threw her against the wall of their other apartment, twice, before Greg could grab her and get her out of there, Greg moved out immediately, also taking Sneezer and everything else in the following weeks, for Greg could be tough when he had to be.

He finally bought Frank a one-way plane ticket away from Denver to get him out of their lives for good. Again, Greg picked up and moved on, finally realizing that living alone was far better than sustaining a bad relationship. Those five months together had seemed like an eternity, but they were over because he had finally willed it.

Chapter Eight

Greg is sitting on the front steps of his apartment building, waiting for Geoffrey, as some random hints of sunlight break in and around the elm trees lining both sides of Humboldt. A light or two is on in his building and in the high-rise across the street. An early morning jogger steadily pads his way down 10th Street to the Park, to circumnavigate its dirt running path. A few of the arboreal squirrels are just beginning to stir on the branches above his head. The promise in the air is of a good day.

Right on time, the silver Trooper pulls up and stops. Geoffrey waves for Greg to join him in the front. Two gorgeous hunks whom Greg has not met are asleep in one another's arms in the back seat. Greg quietly sets his backpack on the floor and closes the door on the passenger side, trying not to make too much noise.

Geoffrey whispers, "The guys in back are Shawn and Mark. They're lovers. I'll introduce you later when they wake up. Neither of them is used to getting up this early, so I'm letting 'em sleep some more."

"Fine," Greg whispers back.

"We'll stop at 'Queen' Soopers to get the water," Geoffrey reminds him.

"Right."

Soon, the two of them are pushing their shopping carts down the aisle of the supermarket.

Greg curiously inquires, "Everyone I've met so far in your group is in a committed relationship. Aren't there any pagans who are single?"

Stopping in the middle of an aisle where rows of bottled water line the shelves, Geoffrey thoughtfully replies, "Not that many, actually. Most of us joined because our boyfriends knew one another. Most guys in relationships know other couples anyway, and we're looking for answers to spiritual questions about life since we already have a life companion. Besides, more of the single guys I know tend to spend much more of their free time looking for a partner, sometimes in the bars; and so they don't have as much time for our movement since we usually head into the mountains on the weekends. Also, contrary to some expectations, we don't have orgies on our encampments. A bunch of single guys might be looking for more than spiritual self-fulfillment in the wilds, I suppose."

"I see," Greg says, loading water bottles into his cart, a touch disappointed, realizing that he probably won't be meeting too many potential boyfriends on this particular outing. He deliberately hadn't brought any condoms or lube with him since he wasn't expecting an orgy, despite his erotic dream the other night. Still, he would at least have liked to meet a few single gay pagans, guys who might want to go out on a date when they aren't in the mountains, worshiping nature.

Since they got an early start, traffic isn't too heavy as they soon drive north and then west.

"I forgot to ask where we're going," Greg admits as they begin ascending into the foothills, well outside of the city.

"We're heading to a spot near the Indian Peaks Wilderness," Geoffrey explains. "The entire area is incredibly beautiful, and a short hike gets us to one peak with a spectacular view, where we can catch the first rays of sunlight coming over the horizon."

After several more miles pass beneath their tires, Greg finally asks what he's been curious to know ever since that PBS fundraiser: "So, tell me about your beliefs. I've read extensively about the Egyptians, the Greeks, and the Romans, especially about their various gods and goddesses and their myths about the origins of the sun and earth and sky. How much of that do you subscribe to?"

Geoffrey readily explains, "First of all, not all of us believe in all of the same things, as you can imagine. Christianity has been around for about 2,000 years now, but paganism had existed in one form or another for thousands of years before that. And, for hundreds of years after the advent of Christianity, paganism had not entirely died out. Most of us do believe in some sort of deity, and that separates us from atheists or agnostics. We simply do not believe that Christ is the Son of God."

"We also don't believe that human beings are stained with original sin." This comment comes from big blond Shawn in the back

25

seat, who had awakened a few miles before and introduced both himself and his partner, Mark.

"We don't believe in *any* concept of sin," Mark firmly adds.

"What about good and evil?" Greg asks.

"That seems to be a very ancient component of many religions, further back even than the pagan Chaldeans who believed that there was a constant battle between good and evil, light and darkness, in the universe," Geoffrey carefully explains.

"But we do believe in a more modern concept of responsibility and irresponsibility," interjects Shawn, hoping to dispel any notion which Greg might have that their paganism lacks an ethical component. "We believe that people act irresponsibly when they are ignorant, either of how their actions will hurt others or how their actions will ultimately hurt themselves."

"You mean, like the ancient Greeks who believed that original sin was a lack of knowledge?" Greg asks.

"Something like that," Geoffrey readily responds. "When people have information, or knowledge, if you will, they are less likely to act irresponsibly, toward others or toward their own better interests. People are often irresponsible only when they incorrectly determine the effects of their behavior on others and the world around them."

"When they steal or kill?" Greg inquires.

"Yes," Geoffrey affirms. "To steal or kill is selfish, self-centered. And all of that behavior is so unnecessary. As we move into the future, technology may likely solve many of our problems by providing for much of our physical needs. People won't need to possess objects or manipulate others for gain because that only limits their spirituality as we discover our true goals in life."

Mark quickly interjects, "The ancient Greeks were not a wealthy people. Their contributions to civilization did not include precious jewelry and fine clothing. They lived more simply so that their need to work was considerably reduced. They could then spend more of their leisure hours stimulating their minds by debating philosophical issues in the Agora, or by watching historical and morality plays in the theater, or by exercising their bodies in the gymnasium."

26

"However," Greg reminds them, "they built their society upon slavery and accorded a second class status to women and to those who were not considered citizens because both of their parents were not citizens of a particular city-state such as Athens."

"True," Geoffrey readily admits. "They also fought amongst themselves, ordered Socrates to commit suicide, tolerated tyrants as rulers, and were prejudicial toward non-Greeks. We aren't defending their errors, or those pagans who did practice human or animal sacrifice, which we abhor. But certain qualities of pagan societies *are* worth preserving. Christianity has attempted to stamp out the responsible as well as the irresponsible in paganism, and we feel that they are wrong to do that."

"What they have substituted is, in too many ways, something much worse," Mark confidently affirms. "Especially when it comes to interpreting the Bible and acting upon those interpretations. There is little or no consistency or rationality, particularly regarding homosexuality."

"I can certainly agree with that," Greg says.

"Jesus Christ said nothing against homosexuals or homosexuality. We all know that. Yet groups like Colorado for Family Values in Colorado Springs and Coach McCartney's Christian men's Promise Keepers movement at CU Boulder use the Bible--their particular interpretation of the Bible--to criticize us terribly, in a most un-Christian way," Shawn indignantly states. "We simply feel that all human beings need to live in harmony with one another and with the Earth around them. Trying to control one another, or harm one another, especially in the name of God, is irresponsible."

"Most importantly," Geoffrey compellingly adds, "we need to focus more of our attention upon *this* existence, this world, and not upon eternal reward or punishment in another life beyond."

"That's one of the biggest difficulties I have with several major contemporary religions, their extreme fundamentalism," Mark indignantly suggests. "Heaven and hell begin to outweigh the Earth and other human beings in their motivation to reap eternal reward."

"Yet most ancient religions, many ancient pagan religions in fact, believed in some sort of afterlife," Greg offers, "no matter how impermanent. Right?"

27

"Right," Mark willingly agrees. "We are not entirely convinced that *this* existence is all that there is. However, the Earth is a living entity. The sun and stars are evolving forms of energy. Without either, we have no existence. They give us life; we have no right to take life from them, to abuse their gifts to us."

"We believe that to spend one's time exclusively in a church with other human beings, to worship God or Christ or whomever, divorces us from the real world," Geoffrey argues. "That form of worship too often separates us from the planet, makes us contemptuous of the soil, the sky, the water, the plants, the animals, even ourselves. We are certainly not above all of those other living things; we are an integral part of life. We might have the capacity to rule over everything, to have 'dominion', as the Bible states; but that does not mean we should always exercise that capacity, or especially exercise it selfishly or maliciously."

"I see," Greg readily concedes. "If we poison a river or the skies to benefit ourselves for some short-term gain, or to satisfy a selfish motive, we are killing ourselves, ultimately."

"Yes," Geoffrey acknowledges. "We should not do so because we are not better--but no worse--than the rocks, the rivers, the skies, the plants, or the animals. All of us have a divine place, a spiritual mission, to perform."

"'The ripped mouse, safe in the owl's talon, cries/ Concordance.'" Greg quotes.

"What's that from?" Geoffrey asks, curious.

"That's from a poem called 'Beasts' by Richard Wilbur. Even though the mouse is soon going to be dinner, he accepts his place in the food chain, if you will, even as he makes the ultimate sacrifice to play that part," Greg thoughtfully explains.

"Yes," Mark willingly nods. "We pagans are not necessarily vegetarians because even a plant, another living thing, is going to be someone's dinner, just like the 'ripped mouse' or insects or cattle eat and then themselves become food."

"Just as you or I," Shawn laughs, "in the wrong place, could end up as some other creature's dinner."

"Nature is neutral, I once told a co-worker," Greg reveals with a smile.

28

"Exactly," Geoffrey replies, his brown eyes mischievously lively. "Whether we're cremated or buried or eaten, for that matter, we ultimately become fertilizer. The life cycle goes on."

Everyone laughs at the truth of that remark.

Greg soon settles back into his seat, knowing that the four of them have probably only scratched the surface of what these modern pagans believe. Besides, he certainly is willing to concede that neither pagans, nor Hebrews, Christians, Muslims, Buddhists, Confucians, Jainists, nor any others in the long history of humanity on Earth, have adopted a belief system strong enough to prevent people, at one time or another, from behaving abominably toward one another or toward the world around them. These pagans simply have yet another interpretation, or perspective, to offer.

Chapter Nine

The campsite is, indeed, beautiful, as Geoffrey had accurately described it. Tall pines entirely encircle it. More than ten small tents are already erected by the time they arrive, all at the edges of the clearing. In the center of this little pagan community, someone has erected a pit for a campfire, using an arrangement of miniature megaliths, looking remarkably like their much larger counterparts, ones that he has seen in so many photographs but never in person. It's a very famous spot, certainly for pagans, in southern England: Stonehenge.

Greg says nothing to the others; but even though this is in daylight, and the other campsite was at night, the setting looks suspiciously like the one he saw in his prophetic dream, just a few nights ago. The slight breeze he now feels is causing the pines to echo the sound one usually perceives by holding up to one's ear a large, chambered shell, flushed from the sea. If ever nature were conspiring to deliver a message, one cautioning him to silence, it is in this motion of countless boughs of mountain trees being pushed into sighing: "Hush."

"Besides," Greg reasons, skeptically gazing at these common surroundings, "one campsite can look pretty much like another."

While helping Shawn, Mark, and Geoffrey unload the Trooper, Greg remembers Joseph's remark the night before about coincidences. "I have to ask him what he means."

When they finish, Greg promises to return to help Geoffrey erect their tent and heads off to find Joseph.

He soon spies Joseph and his partner William in front of a tent on the other side of the encampment, contentedly seated upon campstools.

"How was your ride up here?" Joseph cheerfully asks as Greg approaches.

"Fine," Greg assures him, smiling. "Couldn't have been more interesting."

He then takes an extra seat offered to him and wonders aloud, "Last night, you said that you don't believe in coincidence. I didn't have a chance to ask you what you meant by that."

Joseph chuckles, knowing that these kinds of statements often elicit questions, "Well, we know that coincidences do occur; but we don't believe that they only *seem* to have meaning. A few current writers have dealt with this issue in books such as *The Celestine Prophecy*. However, we primarily take our inspiration, as some of these writers no doubt must have, from the ancients, who were convinced that signs and omens, the flights of birds or the migration of animals, meant something of significance to them. Nearly all pagans have believed that the Earth speaks to them personally about the way that the universe interacts with their lives. Each of us *should* take meaning from any signs that occur for us. Consequently, we believe that every event, every coincidence if you will, occurs for a purpose, whether we are immediately made aware of its meaning or not. For instance, you seeing me on TV last week, and then at Garbo's last night, were meant to happen for a reason. It was not simply a coincidence. Obviously, your being here with us now is proof of that. Two weeks ago, you didn't even know that the Rainbow Arc of Fire existed; today, you're out in the middle of nowhere with us."

"OK," Greg acknowledges, still feeling skeptical but open to being convinced otherwise.

"Look, Greg. We weren't even going to meet at Garbo's; but James, Geoffrey's boyfriend, suggested it before he was unexpectedly called out of town at the last minute. We usually follow through on such suggestions in case the event is supposed to happen for a reason. We believe that we were supposed to meet you at Garbo's, to invite you with us this weekend."

"I'm flattered, but I don't know if that entirely explains it."

"You wanted to learn more about us, right?"

"Right."

"And, as you explained to us last night, you had intended to call the GLCCC to get our number yet failed to do so before we met."

"Yes."

"Then you went to Garbo's, where you almost always go, and we were there."

"Yep."

"Obviously, we were intended to meet all along. Since we do *not* normally go to Garbo's and you do, *our* typical plans were altered to coincide with yours so that we finally met. Perhaps it is because this weekend is intended to be meaningful for all of us, or specifically meaningful for you. We shall see what eventually results."

"Sure. But I'm still not fully convinced."

Patiently, Joseph smiles and continues, "A person must *believe* that coincidences have a purpose, a meaning. They may seem insignificant at first, but then the significance grows as you invest the event with more feeling, more faith, if you will."

He sees that Greg still isn't convinced, so he elaborates, "I'll give you a personal example. I quit smoking a few years ago. I got up one morning determined that I would no longer allow cigarettes to control my life. I had been looking for a lover, unsuccessfully, and felt that my smoking was having a detrimental effect on my search. As the hours and then days passed without a cigarette, I really craved one; but I continued to invest my original decision to quit with more and more meaning. I knew that it would have a positive purpose for my life, even beyond the direct health benefits."

William continues with the story, "We met not long after that. Joseph was in a bar with some friends, but he wasn't smoking. I knew because I watched him. It was important to me that any potential life-partner of mine not be a smoker. My mother used to smoke constantly, but she developed several smoking-related health problems and was finally forced to quit. I refused to get close to anyone who would jeopardize his future for a few moments of nicotine rush."

Joseph adds, "We would *not* have met had I still smoked."

"Again, though," Greg calmly objects, "that meeting could all have been simply a coincidence. Right?"

"Of course, it could," concedes Joseph, realizing that Greg won't likely be persuaded until he experiences some sort of tangible proof for himself. "However, *we* don't believe that it was simply a coincidence because it had meaning for both of us that I had quit. My quitting smoking had a purpose. That purpose was to allow me to meet William and for the two of us to fall in love. Our love is the greatest positive experience in our lives. You cannot convince us otherwise."

"I see," Greg replies, nodding. "In other words, you still must have faith, in a way, to have this belief system work."

"Yes," William quickly chimes in. "Christians are right at least about Faith moving mountains. Our faith, though, has a small 'f' because we don't go out and slaughter or abuse other people for our faith. We try to avoid any negativity regarding others and their beliefs."

"My problem," Greg willingly admits, "is that when I do meet someone under unusual circumstances, and *I* believe that it's Fate bringing the two of us together, the other person never seems to believe it. I *still* end up being single because they move on, ignoring what I thought was something inevitable and special."

"I understand," Joseph sympathizes, having experienced similar disappointments in the past. "That's because *both* participants in an event, or coincidence, have to believe that it is more than simply a random and inconsequential coincidence. When they *do* believe, when they both invest the encounter with meaning, that's when the magic kicks in. Too often, people simply go through life experiencing these little miracles, if you will, and shrug them off. The magic of each of those moments quickly wears off and is gone. It's all rather sad, actually."

"You know," Greg concedes, "sometimes, when someone whom I've met is not interested, and I see him many months, maybe a few years later, he appears regretful that he let the earlier, opportune moment pass. But he seems to know now that it's probably too late."

Joseph nods in agreement, "Yes. It's that old saying, 'You cannot step twice into the same stream.' However, most of the time, those who do let you pass the first time may not have been the right person for you after all. They may have realized, even more than you, that they weren't right because they know themselves better than you do."

Greg purses his lips, contemplating this possibility.

33

Joseph continues, "When you are a decent and kind person, some other people cannot handle it. Especially in the gay community, there is sometimes such low self-esteem regarding how they feel about themselves in relationship to their community, their families, or their straight friends. They think so little of themselves that they often deny themselves the love of someone good, thinking that they should satisfy their needs solely by another's looks, or money, or some other surface quality. Life is reduced, for them, to the shallow or the transitory. It works in a way for some people to live like that because they have few expectations, but it doesn't work for us."

"I've met so many people who seem to undervalue themselves while, at the same time, they go after someone who simply isn't interested. The compatibility is just not there, and they're eternally frustrated," William adds, grateful to have found Joseph after so many previous disappointments.

"One's expectations still have to be realistic," Greg sadly concludes. Then he looks at his watch, "Uh, oh, I better go. I promised Geoffrey I'd help him put up the tent. I gotta run."

"If I know Geoffrey, he won't begin until you arrive. He entirely believes in cooperation, especially when needs are mutual," Joseph smiles, having enjoyed this discussion with Greg immensely even if he senses that Greg has not been entirely convinced, for now.

"You know," adds Greg, "I haven't slept in a tent since Marine Corps Officers' Candidate School in 1972."

"I thought you said that you were in the Air Force," Joseph inquires, puzzled.

"I was. But a year before Air Force Officers' Training School, I was at Marine OCS at Quantico, Virginia; but I hated all that marching in the woods and carrying an M-14 rifle."

"I hope," ventures William with a sly grin, "that your experience this weekend with us will be far more pleasant. We like to think we're not militaristic."

"Right. I'm sure I'll enjoy myself," Greg calls over his shoulder as he hurries off.

He arrives at the tent site, just as Geoffrey is carefully spreading the canvas on the ground.

"You're back sooner than I expected," he tells Greg, standing up and smiling.

"When I found Joseph and William, we started talking about coincidence and stuff like that," Greg confesses sheepishly, realizing how much time they had spent in conversation.

"I thought so," Geoffrey tells him, knowing his two friends quite well after all these years. "That's why I'm surprised you're back so soon. We pagans love a good philosophical discussion."

"I know," Greg grins, shaking his head. "So do I."

Chapter Ten

After Geoffrey and Greg finish putting up the tent, Greg asks him, "Aren't there any lesbian pagans? I haven't seen any women up here. Have you become sexist swine like straight men, excluding women like the Our Gang 'He-man Woman Hater's Club'?"

Geoffrey laughs, not at all offended, "No. We plead innocent. Although there are fewer lesbian pagans, and I have several theories as to why, a few years ago, the women told us that they would prefer to maintain a separate camp. It's not far from here, and we're free to visit one another's camp. We usually have dinner together. We also participate in their Ceremony of the Moon at night, and they will be at our Celebration of the Sun in the morning. Jointly, we conduct the Consecration of the Water and the Earth services this afternoon."

"I guess there are basic differences between men and women that we cannot entirely transcend, whether we're gay or straight," Greg sighs. "The biological differences are the most obvious."

"That seems to be true," Geoffrey concurs. "That's why, although there are exceptions, and it seems less true with younger gays, we still have women's bars and men's bars."

"We also use the terms gay man and lesbian. And some studies seem to reveal that there are fewer lesbians than gay men, whatever the reasons are for that," Greg recalls.

"Yep."

"Oh," Greg interjects, realizing that he's becoming quite hungry, "when's lunch?"

"Soon. Henry and his partner Richard have made their special sub sandwiches, so be sure and make a big fuss," Geoffrey laughs. "Actually, they really are tasty. Others have brought veggies and fruit and chips. Don't forget to keep drinking plenty of fluids. It's easy to get dehydrated up here."

"I'm glad you also told me about the portable toilets. I wouldn't want it to be known that pagan nature worshipers despoil the environment."

"Right," Geoffrey smiles. "It wouldn't do for our image."

After a leisurely and delicious lunch, and a siesta for many of them after, a time that Greg uses to explore the landscape around the camp with Geoffrey, everyone from both camps meets at the nearby stream that runs between the two sites. This gathering, Greg is told, is for the first of the ceremonies, the Consecration of the Water. A small earthen bowl of water, obtained from the Mississippi River by a couple who were at Mardi Gras this past season, after being purified by air and fire earlier, is poured into the stream, to make its circuitous path once again through the nation's heartland.

Joseph and Marina, the tall and silky blond pagan priestess from the lesbian camp, standing upstream from their followers, jointly tip the bowl so that its sacred contents can flow freely past the other pagans.

The two of them chant as they pour: "We send you back upon your long and prosperous journey, Blessing the fertile lands below, Once more to seek your home, the sea, The source of all living entities, So long ago."

Their followers, lining both banks of the stream, join hands across the burbling waters and reply: "We touch and are touched by you, Oh sacred well-spring, Giver of life. Sustain us in our lengthy sojourn toward awareness of ourselves, Renewed."

Greg watches it all with a bemused contentment. The camaraderie is more fascinating to him than any of the ceremonies or the chants, although these, too, are not without a particular charm. Wherever he has gone, whatever he has done, all that he has witnessed in life involves human gatherings of ritual and pomp and circumstance. Even in the military, with its uniforms and rank, its services and ceremonies, awards and salutes, duty and codes of conduct and honor, he has been entertained and often initiated.

For without some sort of elevation, some type of formalized ritual, most human activity could be seen as rather mundane. From raising a barn to launching a ship, from planting a tree to marking the inevitable termination of a life, people sing and dance together, kneel and pray. Celebrations, somber or boisterous, put the appropriate frame upon existence, Greg accepts, creating a beginning or an end,

37

an appropriate border or boundary, to what we experience of our individual selves and our societies.

On their way back to the tent after the Consecration of the Earth, which immediately followed the Consecration of the Water, Greg confesses to Geoffrey, "I feel a little light headed. I've never quite felt like this before."

Not too concerned, Geoffrey advises him, "You're probably just reacting to the altitude. We're several thousand feet higher than Denver, and each person responds differently. Perhaps you should take a nap in the tent. You've been going strong ever since we got here, and you wouldn't want to get altitude sickness."

"You're probably right."

"Besides," Geoffrey explains, an obvious glint of mischief in his eyes, "you wouldn't want to miss the Ceremony of the Moon tonight. The lesbians put on quite a show."

As Greg lies down upon the sleeping bag, he knows that he didn't tell his tent-mate the exact truth. He doesn't feel light-headed so much as he feels light, almost weightless. He remembers vividly how his body experienced fatigue when he first moved to Colorado in 1978. "This sensation isn't at all like that."

"I just need some rest," he tells himself, closing his eyes and quickly dozing off.

This time the dream is more immediately intense. He is looking down as from a great height. He finds himself circling above a mountainous landscape.

"Where am I?" he wonders, feeling that something profound has changed. "What have I become?"

He slowly senses that he is seeing the world through strange new eyes, not his own. Suddenly, he is swept downward through the sky, the Earth looms up so quickly his breath should fly from him; but these are not his lungs breathing. He sees the tiny form scurry beneath. Too late, it is seized.

Now, he finds himself in the grasp of sharp talons, no longer grasping. Slowly, however, as he tries to look up, seeing feathers and a hardened beak, the light of the sun dims and is gone. He sees nothing further and wakes up, in the tent still.

38

He then sits up and looks about himself, confused at these sudden transitions. What did the dream mean? Where was he? Is he wrong even to worry about meaning in an experience such as that one? What kind of effect is this place having on his mind, all of these new circumstances and ceremonies?

He now strangely recalls the time in the Marines when they were required to climb a hugely high ladder pointing to the sky, its thick log rungs bolted to twin steel beams driven firmly into the ground, extending upward certainly three stories, possibly four.

He had always been terrified of falling from any significant height. At the World Trade Center in New York City, even inside the building, he could never bring himself to stand too close to the glass and look down. But in the Marines, forced to scale that height that day, he deliberately started upward, one log at a time. In that platoon of Marine trainees, he banished his fear to the point that, at the very top, where he was required to straddle the uppermost rung and descend on the other side, he paused and looked about. Feeling no fear but only awe, he even looked down at the staff huddled far below. He smiled to himself at this momentary triumph. Then, he comfortably eased himself over the top and started back down.

He feels exactly like that now; and he cannot wait for the Ceremony of the Moon, practically bolting out of the tent for dinner, espying the sacred fire that someone has lighted, its flames dancing in the center of the miniature Stonehenge. Much like the Universe, finite, yet unbounded.

Chapter Eleven

Marina and her girlfriend, Joan, Joseph and William, and Geoffrey and Greg have selected a spot away from most of the others to eat dinner. Balancing their plates of barbecued burgers or chicken, vegetables, rolls, and salad on their knees, they listen to Joan, a deeply tanned woman in her early 40's, with bewitching black hair and eyes, regale them about an experience that she and Marina had earlier in the day, not long after the two Consecration ceremonies.

"We were walking up near the peak when we saw a Bald Eagle in the sky," she tells them, her dark eyes wide with wonder. "It circled for the longest time. Then we saw it swoop down and catch a mouse in its talons and lift off again."

Greg looks up from his plate, intrigued, but says nothing.

Marina, her bright, lively green eyes glinting warmly in the night, describes her conflicted feelings, "I certainly felt sorry for the mouse, but then the eagle must eat to survive. This entire concept of life as a buffet is troubling to me."

She then self-consciously laughs while looking down at her plate, feeling a bit hypocritical, "Here I am gobbling up food that was produced from some kind of living plant or animal."

"I guess," surmises William, emphasizing the humorous side of their situation, "that it's much better to be farther up the food chain than near the bottom."

A few of the others nod in agreement.

"*Our* most worrisome predators these days are among the tiniest forms of life: viruses and bacteria," Joseph practically states, none of them needing to be reminded that he means AIDS and the opportunistic infections that it brings in its wake.

"You're right," Geoffrey sadly agrees, shaking his head as he recalls several dear friends long gone.

"I cannot believe," Marina crossly adds, "that some Christians have dared to say that *any* disease is God's retribution upon any other group of people. So many plagues have been visited upon humankind throughout history. Almost none have ever been any group's *fault*."

"I have always wondered if AIDS might instead be a test of our humanity," Greg quietly tells them, remembering those whom he has known and lost.

"I never thought about it that way," Joan says, reaching over and touching his arm because the remark has deeply moved her. "That's certainly an appropriate sentiment, though."

"Yes, it is," Joseph sadly adds.

They all become silent then, thinking about fallen comrades and friends who might have been with them this night had their life's course gone otherwise.

The fire is still dancing through the trees nearby, casting shadows and making shapes of the looming forms all around them. Voices of the others gathered in the clearing carry past their intimate circle and into the dark forest beyond.

William then speaks up, breaking their somber silence, "It's a beautiful night, isn't it?"

"Yes, it is," Geoffrey quickly replies, looking up at the sky through the pine branches above him. "I keep forgetting how many stars inhabit the night and how many more we can see up here than in the city."

"That's why we come up here so often," Joseph reminds them, his somber mood noticeably brightening, "so we don't forget that the sky is a pagan's roof; the ground, his floor. We have no walls to circumscribe us out here."

Greg tells them, having become quite comfortable in the company of these newly discovered friends, "Ancient men and women hadn't much else to do, outside of their caves or huts in warmer weather, sitting around a campfire after a day of hunting and gathering, but to look up at the sky at night and invent stories about the stars--to explain the complexity of the cosmos and make sense of their seasonal motions across the sky."

"To connect the dots that are the stars and form pictures in their minds to go along with the stories they told," Marina adds, smiling at the thought that they are all carrying out a tradition as old as humanity itself. "It's a pleasure that we have certainly neglected

41

for too long. I wonder if we still would know how to tell stories about the night sky if we were ever suddenly sent back in time, long before technology."

"The only stars that most of us see these days are those on TV and in the movies, with their stories made up for them by professional writers," William chuckles, knowing that they are miles from any television set or theater.

"I wonder," Greg slowly adds, contemplating the possibility, "what it must have been like around those earliest campfires, long before the professional Mesopotamian, Egyptian, and later Greek storytellers had already provided identities and explanations for the various starry forms they saw above them."

"I have often wondered," says Geoffrey, "if it wasn't easier then to be gay, around those earlier campfires. You simply gravitated to the one who attracted you and whom you attracted, without fear of others passing judgment because the rules had not yet been cut into clay or carved in stone by later bigots."

"Your behavior was 'normal' because no one had yet defined it as 'abnormal,' just because everyone else didn't do it," Joan practically adds.

"That is what I most enjoy about being a modern pagan," Marina announces, standing up and reaching her hand out to her partner who grasps it firmly. "We are not bound and gagged by the past. We can improvise."

She pauses for the full effect to be felt, "Wait until you see what we have planned tonight. The old moon will never be the same."

"We await your Ceremony of the Moon with great anticipation," Joseph informs her, smiling at the prospect.

Everyone then carries his or her plate and utensils to the trash bags near the central fire. The women soon head to their camp, to complete their preparations for the night's impending rituals. The men return to their tents to retrieve flashlights for the celebratory hike to the sacred meeting spot.

As Greg watches the others proceed with their several tasks, he instantly forms a profound appreciation of all of them, a sudden flash of insight, as it were, into their various personalities, as if he has

42

known each one for a long, long time. Perhaps this is as much because they have so quickly made him feel welcome and an accepted part of their group, or possibly it is his own intuitive nature at work.

Regardless, he now senses that while Joan may be quick to anger she also seems just as quick to forgive. Marina appears to be the more even-tempered and practical member of that partnership, immediately warm and friendly and caring, toward virtually anyone. William, always outgoing and blithely confident, certainly sees the humor in any given situation and readily points it out, for the enjoyment of the others as well as for his own amusement. Greg has the distinct impression that in school years ago William was likely the class clown. Joseph, by contrast, leads this group as much by example as by his words. There is a gravity and sensibility about him that appears impossible to shake. Geoffrey is that genuine rarity these days, a thoroughly decent guy: no hidden agenda, no profound reservations regarding the world and the people around him, and no deceit.

Enjoying this new experience immensely, Greg happens to look up and notice the large wedge of a moon that has just appeared above the horizon. He then wonders what further surprises and pleasures this night's and the early morning's rituals have in store for him and the others.

Chapter Twelve

Several of the men, carrying flashlights with rainbow-colored plastic cones, fitted on the ends to create a colorful effect, go ahead to mark the trail up to the sacred ground where the Ceremony of the Moon is to take place. They soon stand as sentinels at odd intervals along either side of the winding pathway. The other men, also carrying rainbow flashlights, held aloft like torches, snake their way upward into the otherwise dark night. All are wearing pure white T-shirts since the temperatures are still warm enough. The T-shirts have embroidered rainbow arcs over the left breast.

As their procession reaches a flat, open spot of pebbled ground, they fan out in two directions, left and right, to encircle the rounded site. Making a large circumference of themselves, they hold the rainbow cones of light against their chests. The intense beams shine upwards off their faces, casting an eerie yet pleasing glow.

Several electronic devices are already in place, bathing the circle of pagans with rainbow beams in all directions.

Delighted, Greg whispers to Geoffrey, "Where'd they get those? They're wonderful."

Geoffrey whispers back, "From the *Shocking Gray* catalogue. They are beautiful, aren't they?"

The women follow next in single file. Each is wearing a full silver cape that shimmers and reflects the rainbow arcs of light as the beams sweep around them. Each is also holding a hollow, rainbow-colored arch, cupped piously in her hands and infused with light.

Marina, at the end of the column, is entirely covered in a silver shift. Wearing a shiny silver tiara, a solo crystal featured as the frontispiece, she beams a small shaft of pure white light outward from her forehead. She cradles an impressive crystal arch in her hands. The women, ahead of her, also fan out upon reaching the flat ground, forming a concentric circle within the one made by the men.

A large, flat stone that Greg has only now noticed sits at the center of their two human circles. Marina gracefully steps up onto the flat stone so that everyone gathered below can easily see her.

44

She stands erect and proud, lifting the glowing crystal arch in her hands skyward, toward the massive, bright slice of the moon above.

Exhilarated by the positive energy generated by those around her, she then joyously speaks, her melodic voice resonating into the dark skies above: "We are here to celebrate the Moon, Goddess of the Night. Happy to know that she still yields to our darkness her reflection. Keeper of the Sun's light in His absence, She allows us to know that He is still shinning, now out of our immediate sight, yet safely to return, as He gathers for us once more the approaching dawn. From the very beginning, and for billions of years, She has gently rocked the oceans, the sloshing cradle of tides where life was first nurtured, where life is nurtured still, in the profound depths and the darkness."

The rainbow beams of light from the various chromatic devices have come together, focusing upon the crystal arch that she holds high. At the same time, the moonlight above gently bathes them all in a profound luminosity.

The inner circle of women then steps forward, compressed so that, as their elbows touch, they have formed a tight human circumference around Marina upon the stone. The men also shift their larger circle closer to the center stone as well. With a free arm, each man embraces the one next to him, bonding themselves, each one to the others.

Greg quizzically glances down at the flashlight in his hand. It seems to be vibrating.

"Are you all right?" Geoffrey whispers, sensing the other's sudden preoccupation.

"I think so," Greg whispers back.

Now, however, he realizes that it is his entire body that is vibrating and not the flashlight--as if a thousand tiny fingers were at work, caressing him.

"Do you feel anything?" he asks Geoffrey.

"Like what?"

"Like I'm vibrating?"

Geoffrey turns to look at him, puzzled, "No."

45

"Then forget it," he whispers, surprised and perplexed. "I must be imagining things."

Marina has moved to step down from the center stone, and the two circles of pagans around her recede in waves. The earlier sentinels now descend the path to provide a lighted way once again. First, the column of women file away and break off near the bottom of the trail, to head toward their camp on the left. The men immediately follow them and now turn right toward their own tents.

Someone has gone ahead and re-stoked the fire so that it burns brightly once more. Someone else has turned up a boom box that is playing celebratory dance music, the tune easily recognizable: "We Are Family" by Sister Sledge.

Everyone quickly breaks off into pairs, joyously dancing around the fire. Some of those with big bronzed or hairy chests have taken off their T-shirts, twirling them in the cool air above, in time with the music.

With a wide grin, Geoffrey turns to Greg and asks, "Do you want to dance?"

"Sure," he readily replies, chuckling as they make their way into the midst of the others. It isn't exactly like the dance in his dream, but the spirit of community is still warmly preserved.

As the fire is eventually allowed to die down, everyone slowly moves toward the tents; the music is then extinguished, and the only sounds now are those of the swaying pine forest all around them.

"Try to get some sleep," Geoffrey advises, crawling into his own sleeping bag. "Remember, we still have the final ceremony in the morning."

"Right," Greg yawns, sleepy despite his earlier nap. "The Celebration of the Sun. Can't wait."

Chapter Thirteen

Greg soon finds himself up and sleepily walking, apparently to the portable toilets. The problem is, it isn't he who is walking.

A flashlight points down and illuminates the path being taken. Inside the toilet, someone has written on the back wall: "For a good time, visit Tent #3. --Stan."

Below, someone else has added, "Don't bother. I know Stan, and he's not worth it. --Stan's lover."

When the one who is peeing stops, turns, opens the door of the portable toilet, and walks back in the direction of the tents, Greg still cannot determine whose eyes he's peering through, feeling very much like a voyeur. He is certainly in the men's camp, that much is certain. As the walking figure stops at a familiar tent flap, Greg is pretty sure where he is. The tent flap is thrown open, and Greg sees the disconcerting figure of himself, lying in a sleeping bag on the floor of the tent. Now, he knows that he's been piggybacking Geoffrey's eyes. How is it possible? This has simply got to be a really weird and vivid dream.

"Greg!" Geoffrey whispers, leaning over, "It's almost time to get up. Are you still sleeping?"

The piggybacking instantly ceases.

"If you shine your flashlight in my eyes, I won't be asleep," Greg laughs, remembering the night his Marine Corps OCS tent-mate, a lumbering Gomer Pyle type from North Carolina, actually shined a flashlight directly into his face to ask if he were asleep.

Rolling over, still groggy but trying not to sound too unsettled, Greg slowly opens his eyes and asks, "How was your walk to the toilet?"

"Fine," Geoffrey replies, surprised. "How did you know?"

Greg thinks fast, "Where else would you be at this hour? Is it light outside yet?"

"No, of course not," Geoffrey reflexively laughs at the absurdity of the question. "We have to get up to the peak *before* the sun comes up. That's the whole point of the Celebration of the Sun, silly."

"I forgot," Greg smiles, wanly, since he knows he isn't very good at impromptu excuses.

"Want me to get you some coffee?"

"I don't drink coffee. If there's some orange juice, I'll take some."

"I'm sure there is. Henry and Richard are probably already up, and breakfast is just about prepared, if I know the two of them."

"Fine," Greg yawns, still feeling a bit unsettled. "Just give me a minute to locate my jeans and I'll join you."

"OK. Meet you in the kitchen."

After Geoffrey leaves, Greg fishes around for his Levis. Fortunately, he left his ceremonial flashlight near his sleeping bag. "As long as I don't find any spiders around here, I'll be fine," he says aloud, flashing the light nervously about the tent floor.

"Ah, there are my jeans."

He crouches in the low tent and puts them on, after shaking them vigorously, hoping that anything that might have crawled into them during the night will flop out and scurry away before he inserts his legs.

He is still avoiding any deliberate contemplation of his latest dream since he feels less and less certain that these experiences in his sleep *are* dreams. However, he determines to walk directly to the one portable toilet that he hasn't used to confirm something.

The hard ground crunches noisily under his feet as he crosses the spacious compound. Opening the door after knocking and hearing no reply, he points his light at the far wall. There, exactly as he dreamed, or rather just as he saw through Geoffrey's eyes, is the graffiti exchange penciled by Stan and his boyfriend.

"Damn," he sighs, still reluctant to accept an inevitable explanation for what is happening to him. "I was hoping I'd find a blank wall."

He backs out slowly, almost tripping on the lower step while letting the door slam shut. Fortunately, it's too dark for anyone to notice the bizarre look on his face.

48

Chapter Fourteen

Not long after an uneasy breakfast, uneasy for Greg at least, everyone from both camps is expectantly gathered on the crest of the nearby peak. Joseph holds a large crystal prism between his outstretched hands in anticipation. Fortunately for Greg, all of the others are simply gathered randomly around him, paying more attention to the distant horizon than to one another.

He deliberately holds back, not so certain that he wants to complete this final ritual initiation. His mind has been racing in circles ever since he was confronted by the writing on the portable toilet wall.

During breakfast, wondering why his new companion has grown so obviously silent and preoccupied, a curious Geoffrey had asked, "Are you all right?"

Greg immediately waved off his question, "I'm fine. Really. Just can't wait for the final ceremony." He was lying through his teeth.

Although Geoffrey did not really buy his friend's unlikely explanation, he asked no further questions.

"Here it comes," someone shouts as the first, intense beam of sunlight shoots toward this cluster of pagans, expectantly huddled on a chilly mountaintop.

Their eyes bright with wonder, each one of them feels as if he or she is the first man or woman conscious of his own existence, watching the initial rays of that early planetary sun, stirring their minds and vision as never before.

The bright beam of light appears to focus upon the prism in Joseph's hands, striking it and shattering itself into a glorious rainbow effect. Greg tries to duck the intense refracted energy that appears to be aimed directly at him; but he is instantly struck, and this arc of many colors fully envelops him.

Everyone else instantly turns in profound amazement to see this clear sign of tremendous wonder. A beatific aura then forms to

49

the contours of Greg's body. He looks about at the others as if through a sparkling cloud and is transfixed.

"Happens to me every time," he laughs, hollowly.

Each of them is too stunned for the moment to respond. And no one, not even Greg, feels threatened by this marvelous display.

Relentlessly, the orange ball of the sun eases itself up over the horizon, now virtually unnoticed by the small band of astonished pagans. In all of this intensifying light, the aura around Greg soon dims and then fully diminishes, as if absorbed by his very skin. Then it is entirely gone.

"All right!" exclaims one of the women, nodding appreciatively. "Neat special effect."

The others almost involuntarily break into applause.

A startled Joseph has forgotten his intonation, but nobody notices. Several are patting Greg on his back, congratulating him on this visual coup. He still looks rather bewildered.

"It's a glorious morning," Marina tells them all, never one to deny the significance of any miraculous event that takes place in their midst.

"It certainly is," Joseph seconds her, curiously glancing down at the prism in his hand while shaking his head in palpable wonder.

Soon, on their way back down from the mountaintop, Geoffrey finally asks Greg, "How did you do that?"

"Trade secret," he nervously responds, trying for a sophisticated intonation but achieving far less.

"Well," Geoffrey continues, unsure if there could *be* a plausible explanation for what they all had just experienced, "That was the most awesome sight I have ever witnessed up here."

"Thanks," Greg awkwardly grins, wondering what in the heck is going to happen to him next.

Chapter Fifteen

After the Celebration of the Sun, several of the others retire to their tents to nap for a couple of hours before all of them pack up after lunch and return to the city. Greg determines that he is not going to allow himself any opportunity to dream, at least for the time being, until he figures out what this latest energizing has done to him. He still feels a profound tingling, especially inside his head.

Richard, who has been running the makeshift kitchen for every meal of their brief stay, has made him a cup of hot chocolate and brings it over, along with a cinnamon roll, "Here you are, Hon. You sit right there and enjoy your hot cocoa. Then, you can tell Auntie Richard all about it."

He plops himself into a chair next to Greg, patting his arm. With his dark brown eyes, he looks deeply into Greg's own, expecting an answer.

"About what?" Greg mumbles, biting into the heated roll and feigning innocence.

"You know what I'm talking about," Richard sighs, tossing his gray head back with a laugh. "What happened to you up on the peak this morning!" he whispers, conspiratorially. "That wasn't any special effect now, was it?"

"No," Greg ruefully admits, deflated, setting the roll down on his plate. "To tell you the truth, I don't know *what* has been happening to me ever since I first heard about you pagans on TV."

"Well, then, just start at the beginning," Richard implores, savoring the moment. "Don't leave out a thing! Then, maybe I can help you sort out all of this craziness. I've been watching you ever since we arrived, and I knew something special was going on."

Reassured, Greg smiles. He then proceeds to tell him about the first dream that he had at home after seeing Joseph on the PBS fundraiser. He finally concludes his strange tale by filling Richard in on the experience earlier with the portable latrine.

"So, you see," concludes Greg, summing up the situation rather grimly, "I have no idea *what* I'll experience next or *why* I've been experiencing any of this."

"We have been coming up here for years," Richard confesses, easing back into his folding chair with an audible sigh. "Henry just loves this mumbo-jumbo stuff. Me?"

He then conspiratorially leans closer and whispers softly, "I think it's all just a teensy bit silly. But don't ever breathe a word of that to Henry or the others! I do love to prepare food, especially for all these flaming pagans."

He then leans back once more, laughing, "We've become like one big family."

"I know what you mean," Greg nods, taking a deep gulp of warm chocolate and then squishing a soggy marshmallow against the roof of his mouth.

He then asks, "Have any of the others experienced anything like this on your previous outings?"

"I have never," Richard replies, carefully emphasizing each word, "never seen nor heard *anything* like what you've told me."

"Oh," Greg says, feeling a bit downcast that he's the only one.

"Not that I don't believe all that you've told me. I do."

Richard pats Greg's arm again and continues, "My family is Cajun, on my momma's side. What she has told me about what goes on in the Bayous of Louisiana would stand your hairs straight up-- even the ones that aren't gray."

Greg laughs in spite of himself.

"But let me tell you," Richard practically adds, "what you are experiencing sounds to me like a gift."

"A gift?" Greg responds, highly doubtful.

"You bet," Richard quickly assures him. "Those witch doctors living on the Bayou consider their powers a gift. Someone or something is giving *you* a mighty powerful gift, my friend."

He slaps his hands on his thighs for emphasis, "Now, I can't tell you what it all means, or what the heck you're going to do with it; but I would highly recommend that you look upon what's been happening as a *gift* and be grateful for it."

52

Greg still looks skeptical, so Richard continues, "Look, Greg. It's probably going to be like any other kind of talent that humans develop. Either you use it right, or you lose it!"

He puts his arms around Greg and gives him a reassuring hug, "It'll be fine, really."

Then he stands up with an air of finality, "I got to get back to my kitchen. You just keep me posted, OK? Especially if you start communicating with the dead, anything like that."

He then widely grins, "Just kidding."

"I'll keep you up to date on my condition," Greg smiles at the older man, grateful for the reassurance. "I promise."

Chapter Sixteen

After Richard leaves, Greg gets up and walks away from the camp, spending the next few minutes strolling through the woods, to be by himself, contemplating what this 'gift,' such as it is, means to him. He cannot understand how useful it will be to look at the world through the eyes of animals and other humans, especially when he seems unable to control what he sees or through whose eyes he looks. Besides, he realizes, these random experiences have only occurred when he's asleep.

"I'd be in heaven if I were a peeping Tom," he admits, ruefully considering that possibility.

Lost in thought, he suddenly stops on the trail. Incredible as it seems to him, he's not only looking through someone else's eyes at this moment he now "hears" that person's thoughts.

"Whoa!" he says aloud, closing his own eyes to focus on this startling development.

He finds himself looking at another guy. He immediately recognizes Shawn, seductively sitting on a rock. The person whose eyes he is "borrowing" is contemplating what Greg delicately defines as lascivious activity.

"I certainly hope this is Mark," Greg chuckles, although his attempt to determine whose thoughts he is eavesdropping is blocked by the lust he senses in the other's mind.

He also feels extremely embarrassed and guilty that he is eavesdropping on someone he knows, "If I were not being a voyeur before, I certainly am now!"

The eyes he is seeing through look down at the muscular, blond Shawn, head tilted back in the morning light. The two then embrace and kiss. The one's thoughts continue to exhibit pure passion. Greg sees fevered hands reach for Shawn's leather belt and loosen it. Then, a tank top is lustily drawn over Shawn's head, revealing a rippled torso. Finally, those same strong hands reach down Shawn's lower back, feeling for firm buttocks. Greg cannot see this last part. He feels it instead. Apparently, the other has closed his

54

eyes and is yielding to his tactile senses. Greg feels the hiking shorts being pulled off.

"Enough!" Greg shouts, finding himself instantly aroused.

The link breaks.

Greg looks about himself, once again unfettered.

"Talk about virtual reality!" he nervously giggles. "I mean, this is fabulously erotic and sensual, but I don't think it's what I'm supposed to do with this 'gift.' I feel like a high-tech pervert."

Nervously, he resumes walking, resisting mightily the urge to peep once again. He now sees a small clearing up ahead.

"Whoops!" he tells himself, veering along a different path when he sees two entirely naked men, making love to one another on a boulder in that clearing.

"I'm glad that it *was* Mark," he says, relieved, having gotten away without being caught spying. "It's bad enough to catch people in the act in your mind. It's far worse to actually catch them in the flesh."

A few yards further down this new trail, he stops suddenly. He now senses pain. He looks down at himself, startled. He realizes that it isn't his own pain that he feels. Whose pain? Where?

He begins walking quickly in the direction that he feels is correct. Not far, he stops and listens. Someone is calling aloud for help.

Almost reflexively, he tries to make contact with the other using his thoughts, "*I'm coming. Don't move!*"

The other person is startled, looking about, wondering where the voice she hears in her head is coming from.

Greg ignores her puzzlement and keeps moving in her direction.

Just off the trail ahead, he sees a woman holding her ankle. She is one of the lesbians he hasn't met but recalls having seen during the Ceremony of the Moon last night.

"I'm here," he calls out, waving.

She looks up, relieved that someone has found her. "I didn't think that anyone would come looking for me this soon. I was walking down this path daydreaming and slipped. I was so stupid not to be more careful."

55

Greg bends down to look at her ankle and sees that it's badly swollen. "We must get it elevated," he orders. "I don't have any ice."

"It really hurts," she complains, grimacing as a tear comes to one eye.

"I know," he says, and he means it. He senses exactly what she's feeling.

He gently elevates the leg. An idea then comes to him: he tries to siphon her sense of pain, hoping that this can work like anesthesia.

"That feels much better," she tells him, moments later, smiling for the first time.

"Good."

He thinks to himself, "It works!" But he has to admit, "We need some ice."

He has another idea that he feels is worth a try. "Whom should I attempt to contact?" he asks himself.

He realizes that Richard is the only one who won't be completely startled. He concentrates his thoughts upon Richard. Suddenly, he finds himself looking through the eyes of someone standing at a camp stove, holding cooking utensils.

"*Richard!*" Greg pleads, making contact. "*It's Greg. Listen to me. A woman has hurt her ankle and needs ice and a way to get back to camp. We're on a trail leading south of camp.*"

He senses that Richard is confused, "*I don't have time to answer your questions. Just get some ice and some help. Please hurry!*"

He knows that Richard still is puzzled, but he also senses that he is getting help.

Greg turns again to the woman, "What's your name?"

"I'm sorry, it's Jill," she tells him, grateful for his presence.

"My name's Greg," he tells her. "It was a good thing that I happened along."

"Yes," Jill admits, relieved. "I don't know how long I would have waited if you hadn't arrived."

56

Greg remembers that Shawn and Mark are not far away; but when he considers contacting them for help, he realizes that they are still "busy."

"Besides," he tells himself, "they don't have any ice."

A few minutes later, Greg senses that Richard and some others are approaching, "I think I hear someone coming."

"Oh, good."

He calls out, "Help!" This is for Jill's benefit.

Richard soon appears, carrying a large bag of ice and an Ace bandage. He is followed by two women and two men, carrying a makeshift litter.

"Got your message," Richard says in a low voice, winking.

"Great!" Greg whispers.

One of the men, a nurse, takes over. Soon, Jill is being carried down the path to the camps, her ankle wrapped in ice.

"I'm glad nobody asked any questions," Greg confides to Richard as the two of them bring up the rear.

"Me, too," Richard says in a low voice. "I just told them that we had an emergency and they took off with me, no questions asked about how I knew."

"They probably just assumed that you'd come across her yourself," Greg laughs.

"Right. Everyone is willing to help out in an emergency," Richard agrees.

"I'm not ready to explain any of this yet, to anyone," Greg reveals.

"I understand," Richard nods. "But you do have to admit, this gift is getting more interesting all the time."

"Indeed it is," Greg sighs. "Far more than I ever imagined."

Chapter Seventeen

After lunch, the ride back into the city is uneventful, fortunately for Greg. Shawn and Mark are again sleeping in the back seat.

"No wonder," Greg smiles to himself, envious, "after their little afternoon 'recreation.'"

Greg is relieved that Geoffrey's mind is focused on his driving, or on his absent boyfriend, James, whom he misses terribly.

"So, James is a corporate jet pilot?" Greg asks, absentmindedly.

"What?" Geoffrey responds, looking up from the monotonous roadway. "Oh, yes. He is. He got called for a flight at the last moment, so that's why he couldn't come with us. This is the first Summer Solstice that we've not been to together for several years."

"I see," Greg says, catching himself for almost saying, "I know," since he's used much of this travel time to try out his newfound abilities as the miles pass by them outside.

Once, a ground squirrel on the roadside ahead almost darted out onto the highway. It surely would have been hit by the Trooper. Greg mentally ordered it to stay put and smiled down at the confused little critter as they zoomed by.

Animals don't think at all in words, he realizes, wondering why he should be surprised by that revelation. Humans, on the other hand, he determines, sometimes think in words, even whole sentences, but just as often merely in partial concepts, refracted visions, and fragmented images of the present and the past, commingled. They even imagine the future, events they want to have occur or events they expect will occur. Their thoughts wander, randomly, making it difficult to always predict what they'll think of next, or what they'll do.

He's never quite realized how undisciplined human thought processes are, even his own, until he began sampling the thoughts of others.

Using Geoffrey, Shawn, and Mark, as well as an occasional, passing motorist, he tests his abilities carefully, fascinated by the simplicity of human thought patterns whether they are awake or dreaming. They seem entirely unaware of his mental browsing, but he is virtually certain that they would expressly resent his intrusions, were they to find out what he is capable of. Fortunately, too, he finds that his ability to read minds does not extend outward indefinitely. He tries to find and contact close friends of his in Denver and comes up with nothing.

"I obviously don't work like a cellular phone," he reasons.

He is most relieved to discover that he actually can control when he piggybacks another's vision or reads another's thoughts, for he recalls another favorite poem by Richard Wilbur, "The Mind Reader." In it, the main character *can* read minds. Unfortunately, his mind seems to be continuously bombarded by the thoughts of those about him. Therefore, he forms a low regard of others simply because of this ungovernable ability to hear them thinking their every thought, no matter how low or mean-spirited. In order to shut out their petty demands, selfish desires, and the low esteem he has for his peers, he drinks. It helps only a little.

"I don't drink," Greg reminds himself, thankful for that and that he doesn't have difficulty tuning out others. He simply doesn't tune them in.

"Where's the catch?" he wonders, as he looks about the vehicle at the others, who are entirely unaware that he now knows many of the most intimate details of their lives, almost by accident, certainly by forgivable curiosity.

Having developed a healthy suspicion of anything that seems favorably to have come his way, he recalls countless books, movies, television shows, legends, and myths that have depicted experiments gone awry, people made mad by helpless transformations, needs unmet and turned ravingly vicious, whenever puny beings exceed their base abilities and step into uncharted territory: Werewolves, vampires, invisible men, wanton telepaths, and scarred monsters are, all of them, typically raging with uncontrollable power and anger and fear.

"Only in comic books," he ponders to himself, "do some characters with superhuman powers react favorably." Of course, he also recalls, many of *them* turn to evil, abusing their fantastic abilities selfishly, threatening mankind and one another with ultimate destruction. For every super-heroic being, dozens of supervillains spring up, virtually a new one every issue or so, he remembers. Even in mythology and literature, Thor has his Loki; Perseus his Medusa; Dorothy her Wicked Witch.

On which side of the heroic pinnacle will he fall, he wonders? Will he join the Heroes' Pantheon or that of the Villains?

He likes to think of himself as a decent person, a generous human being. But so, too, he remembers, did many others in history who at one time or another found themselves in lofty possession of eminent prestige, economic control, or personal performance. "...Absolute power corrupts absolutely," he reflects. Is that merely an aphorism, or something more telling?

What would he have done, he speculates, had he been able to read the mind of that tormented, confused, yet devious and sociopathic, Academy cadet who ruined his military career so thoroughly and so long ago? How would he have reacted to those Air Force special agents who first listened to the preposterous lies told about him and believed them, who greedily read his most intimate thoughts put to paper for the first time in those revealing and especially intimate letters to the cadet, and who then became overtly willing coconspirators in his personal tragedy?

All these years later, he still feels such intense anger, such humiliation, welling up at what he suffered back then. All of that mortification simply because the authorities discovered he is gay.

He doesn't particularly care for how he still feels, at this particular moment, all of these many years later. Yet, ominously, he knows that he now has the power to do something about it.

Chapter Eighteen

Geoffrey stops in front of the apartment building on Humboldt Street. Greg grabs his backpack, steps out of the Trooper, says good-bye to everyone; and the others drive off. He waves until the silver vehicle moves down the block, stops at the sign on 9th, turns left toward the Park, and is gone.

He pivots to walk up the steps to the lobby but senses that he is being observed. He glances up into the trees above him and notices that on several branches, a number of squirrels are now watching him, obviously curious. One, an especially brave fellow, descends and approaches him on the sidewalk, tail twitching.

Greg sits down on the concrete walk and begins to communicate with this furry ambassador from the neighborhood, fascinated to learn that these small creatures already sense something profoundly different about him. He tries looking at himself through the eyes of the squirrel, sampling the little guy's senses, to understand more fully how it is that they are aware of him. He is startled to realize that they see him almost akin to a miniature sun, much dimmer of course, but beaming a subtly warm glow, an aura, like that which comes at them massively from above, through the branches and leaves of the tree-world they inhabit.

Probing further, he realizes that they are far more motivated by their simpler hierarchical desires like gathering food and eating, sleeping, and reproducing, than the humans whom he'd sampled earlier. Self-preservation seems of paramount importance to squirrels at all times.

Even now, as a car zooms by on the street, the squirrel sitting in front of him is concerned. Greg, however, notices that the driver is eyeing him peculiarly. He looks around to see that several other squirrels and even a few birds have gathered about him.

"This is like some damned Disney movie," he laughs, getting up awkwardly from the sidewalk, though trying not to startle or step on any of his newfound acquaintances, while trying to explain to this curious menagerie that he must return to his own living quarters and

61

that they should do likewise. They seem to understand the concept of a dwelling place, but they do not comprehend his motivations for going indoors.

He waves good-bye but knows that they certainly don't understand what this friendly, human gesture means.

He checks his mailbox in the lobby, unlocks the inner door to the courtyard, and then heads up the stairs to his apartment on the second floor. Even now, he senses that his cats are aware of his return, for they again await him at the front door.

This time, they seem to regard him differently, "Hello, Sneezer. Hi, Schnozz. You guys hungry?"

He senses that they are hungry and goes to the refrigerator to get their food. Dumping two containers, one into each bowl, he stands back.

Sneezer dives in. Schnozz eyes him momentarily. "Go ahead, Schnozz, eat," he orders. "It's still me."

He picks up the Sunday newspaper that Ramsey obviously set inside the door earlier in the day. He eyes the typical headlines but then his sight reflexively trails along to the lower corner of the front page, "Oh, my!"

Nervously, he gets up, nearly stumbling over the two cats who have finished eating and are sitting attentively on the floor, looking up at him.

"What?" he demands, realizing that, in his excitement, he probably spoke louder than he intended.

Hoping for forgiveness, he stoops to pick each one up, hugs it, and places it back down on the carpet. They have never understood this gesture, he now realizes.

Perplexed, he grabs the white legal envelope from off of the refrigerator and pulls out the familiar printed tickets.

Sitting back on the couch to steady himself, he carefully compares the third row on the ticket with the numbers in the newspaper. "They're the same!" he excitedly thinks.

Still unconvinced, he reaches for the phone, dialing the number listed on the back of the ticket.

The computerized voice on the other end confirms the numbers printed in the paper.

"I forgot how much it's worth," Greg says to the cats.

He reaches for the Saturday paper, flipping through the second section. On the third page, in a full-page Lotto ad, is the familiar phrase: "$15,000,000! Is that enough for you?"

"You bet," he animatedly says, jumping up and grabbing each cat again and hugging it.

"We're rich!" he exclaims, dancing around the room until he senses a profound discomfort in Sneezer, who doesn't enjoy this physical celebration. He instantly stops dancing.

"I'd try and explain winning the lottery to you," he laughs, giddy with the news, "but I don't see how you'd understand the concept of money."

Sitting down again, he tells them, "I feed you the best food I can get. You have enough cat toys, and I indulge your whim to hang around outside the front door. I change your litter boxes every week. I don't know what else I can do for you two."

Suddenly, Greg realizes, "I have to call Mike in California."

He grabs the phone and dials.

He and Mike have known one another for 30 years, first sitting one behind the other in Mr. Ivan's 9th Grade English class at South Gate Junior High School in 1964. It was in the fall as freshmen in high school when the two became friends, later attending the same colleges. Greg was best man at Mike's wedding not long after graduation. He was also there on the turmoil-filled night when Mike told his wife that he is gay. Greg was also at Mike's side when Mike tearfully scattered the ashes of his partner of nine years at sea two months ago.

The two have a lot of shared history between them.

The phone rings at Mike's end and he answers.

"Mike, it's Greg. You won't believe this, but I just won the Colorado Lottery!"

He figures this news will be easier for Mike to believe than what he also will tell him.

"How much? Fifteen million! But that isn't the biggest news," he confesses.

"No," he quickly demurs, "I haven't met anyone who is interested."

63

He pauses, trying to come up with the right way to put this, "It's much bigger than meeting someone, actually; but I'm not really sure how you're going to believe me."

He looks down at his two cats, stumped.

"Look, Mike, remember when I called you Friday night and told you about going up into the mountains with those pagans this weekend? Well, that's where it all started."

Chapter Nineteen

It takes all of Greg's persuasive abilities, and all of their 30 years of friendship, for Mike even to begin to accept what he is told, especially since the excessive distance prevents Greg from proving what he can do.

"Besides," Greg eventually tells him, "I don't intend to read the minds of my friends unless a situation arises that absolutely requires it. This can certainly be a terrible invasion of someone's privacy."

After eventually hanging up the phone, Greg ponders the ethical dilemma that he faces. Fortunately, Mike has always been a good sounding board for him. That was why Greg was determined to tell him. Richard also knows, but Greg is certain that he can be trusted not to say anything, even to Henry.

Greg reasons to himself, "Imagine trying to tell anyone that you know someone who can read minds and influence behavior. Who'd believe you? Especially if I refuse to provide proof of my abilities?"

Greg smiles inwardly, "People would think that the other person is nuts."

As he later readies himself for bed, he reflects further upon another predicament that he and Mike discussed earlier. Mike thought that being able to read minds might help Greg meet someone who is interested, "You could easily find out if he's genuinely interested in a potential long-term relationship or just a one-night stand."

Greg countered that argument with another concern, "Do I really want to know *exactly* what someone thinks of me? I mean, if I see someone whom I'm interested in and want to confirm if he's interested in me, I may encounter some random thoughts that I really would rather not read."

"I see what you mean," Mike realized. "I wouldn't want to discover that the other person thinks I'm a total troll."

"When you read someone else's mind," Greg advised him, "you unfortunately get the complete truth of what's in another's thoughts at the moment. It could be that he thinks you're a troll. It might also be that he thinks you're a hot stud but nothing more."

"Right." Mike readily agreed. "You're nothing but a piece of meat on a rack."

"That's it," Greg told him. "Objectively, it might be nice for about five seconds to be thought of as a sex object. Over the long run, I'm not so sure that being thought of like that is beneficial."

Once in bed, the lights out, the city humming fitfully outside his window, Greg looks up at the street lamp glow on the ceiling above. From the apartment building across the alley in back, he suddenly hears a terrible row begin between a couple living there. Not only is the argument noisy, with all of the yelling that Greg easily hears, but it also seems threatening, with shouts and counter shouts, soon escalating. He sits up, worried. Some of the angry thoughts that also come wafting, heatedly, out their windows and through his window, are not pleasant. They are, in fact, far scarier to him than the nasty verbal epithets that the two recklessly hurl at one another.

In response, his mind widely sweeps through the streets of the neighborhood, down one block and up another. He searches for the right agent to handle this situation, while fervently hoping that he finds him in time.

Shortly, he does locate him; or rather, her. A few, covert suggestions, and the police cruiser has turned down 10th Street, the driver's window open to the fullest sounds of an intensely warm evening. The officer hears the vocal disturbance immediately, as Greg intended that she would, and stops her vehicle. She opens the car door, gets out, tucks her nightstick into her belt, and walks toward the front lobby of the building.

Only then does Greg work to soothe the fraying edges of a relationship turned quarrelsome and bitter, over what he senses is so little, made much too large and cumbersome over time.

A few minutes later, the ruckus having subsided, the officer returns to her vehicle and drives off.

"It's like having a mental discussion, a debate if you will, with yourself," Greg realizes, thinking about the techniques he employed throughout the incident. People's wandering thoughts entertain suggestions on a hot night, with no single idea particularly pressing, in the case of the police officer. From the deep recesses of the other's mind, who is to know the source of a particular directive when one is receptive to randomly changing course? By turning a police car down one particular block instead of another, Greg has the right person take the proper course of action toward handling a domestic dispute that the officer might otherwise have heard about too late.

Then, by causing recriminations to subside by bringing each combatant to his or her senses, by disengaging their anger or redirecting it, he could slowly urge the couple back to a truer sense of themselves, before each lost all self-control. Very much like turning down a thermostat or a burner on a stove, he must do so gradually, he recognizes, so that no one is the wiser.

"This power can be made to work with utmost subtlety," Greg acknowledges to himself.

Within the vibrating walls of the other apartment, once white hot but growing increasingly cool, one quietly says to the other, now subdued, "I don't know why I was so angry."

"Me either. I'm sorry that I lost my temper," the other says, repentant. "I feel really embarrassed that the police had to stop by."

"I agree. You know that I love you."

"I love you, too."

In the calm aftermath, each finally agrees to seek counseling. A relationship such as theirs is too valuable, they soon acknowledge to one another, to allow temporary arguments and potential violence to ruin it irretrievably when help exists.

Free at last to sleep, a relieved Greg turns over and begins to descend into a peaceful respite, telling himself, "I doubt if other conflicts that I encounter will be quite so easy to referee."

Chapter Twenty

The next morning, Greg calls his team leader at BMI to tell him that he will not be in today since he has an annuity check worth possibly $250,000 to pick up at lottery headquarters downtown. After the team leader gets over the sudden shock, Greg promises that he will not quit immediately and leave them in a lurch when product announcements are heavy.

As he hangs up the phone, Greg feels suddenly elated that he will never have to work again for the rest of his life, unless he chooses to. He knows that the annuity checks will arrive once a year for the next 25 years, increasing at the rate of 3.7 percent annually.

"Financial freedom!" he loudly shouts, exhilarated at the prospect. Sneezer and Schnozz give a start.

The question he asks himself, however, "Is this all a coincidence?"

He's played the state lottery for four years; why did he win now? While he was undergoing these amazing mental transformations up in the mountains, the magic combination of numbered Ping-Pong balls was popping up in his favor in Denver. He now has money enough not to work if he doesn't want to. Or should he phrase it thus: When he *needs* to take time off for some significant reason, he can afford to?

Now that he has won all of this money, maybe he's not supposed to spend it selfishly. He speculates that it's too much of a coincidence that he's won on the same weekend that he's gained these impressive powers. If the two miraculous events are somehow connected, he'd better not spend it as if it's all his to squander however he wishes.

He is someone who has always lived rather simply. He vows not to change his spending patterns. He can pay off what bills he has. Beyond that, he realizes that he should be financially cautious. If not a coincidence, this odd combination of events has been altogether rather convenient.

"We'll see what happens," he says, relieved nonetheless.

Before he leaves his apartment, he calls the phone company to request a new, unlisted phone number. This is a result of warnings he has read about in the newspaper from other lotto winners if you don't want to be inundated with calls from those wishing to spend your money for you. They also advise, "Don't feel bad about saying 'No' to requests for money. You cannot help everyone."

"Well, maybe not," Greg smiles, considering some of the more intriguing possibilities. "Then, again, maybe now I can help in my own, unique way."

He stands at the mirror in the bathroom, putting on glasses that he normally never needs to wear, after combing his hair differently and leaving the stubble on his chin that grew during his mountain sojourn. He knows fully well that winning this kind of money in Colorado, where the jackpots almost never get much higher, gets your picture in the paper and your visage on the local news. He doesn't want to look too much like himself during these media sessions so that he'll be less recognizable afterwards. He prefers as much anonymity as possible now that he may very well need something approaching a secret identity regarding his new abilities.

Later, at lottery headquarters, he endures the lengthy wait for the paperwork to be completed. He then handles meeting the press with aplomb. When asked what he intends to do with all of that money, he coolly replies, "Spend it." This garners a hearty laugh from the envious throng.

Envy is an emotion that Greg fully understands since he's wanted to win for years. Also, living alone in a world that values relationships makes one quite envious.

He used to worry that winning the lottery would make him even more cautious than he has already become about meeting new people. How would he know that another man were interested in him and not solely in his newfound riches?

Now, he will know.

After he finally gets the first check and leaves lottery headquarters, he immediately heads for his bank to deposit the money. Reaching outward with his powerful thoughts as he passes by several employees and bank managers, he gets no sense inside the building that this financial institution is headed for any kind of economic debacle any time soon. He feels even more comfortable, knowing that the money will be safe.

He then drives down Colorado Boulevard for the freeway and the on-ramp heading south to Colorado Springs and the Air Force Academy, his primary objective this day.

Years before, in his anger and bitterness, his pain and profound sense of loss, he had imagined himself someday garbed in camouflage and hauling heavy weapons, stalking those who had wronged him down the long, narrow, marble corridors of the Administration Building, Harmon Hall. There would be no escape for the guilty then, or now.

Tossing grenades left and right into offensive and officious offices, firing his assault rifle copiously as his dark, shiny boots thudded mightily across the slick and blood-spattered floors, he visualized himself plugging special agents and guilty Air Force officials with a vengeance and without remorse, letting secretaries and the other innocents caught in the cross-fire go free.

"I was just doing my duty," he would subsequently, and grimly, tell the surviving authorities who would ask, heads shaking, why he precipitated such a senseless massacre as they accepted his unconditional surrender.

Of course, that form of revenge was all in his head.

Although he had qualified in both the Marines and the Air Force with a variety of combat weapons, he's never owned a gun nor ever wanted to. He is aware that the newspapers are filled nearly every month with accounts of disgruntled current and former employees, often working for the Post Office, who slaughter co-workers and bosses over slights far milder than those which he endured. Although provoked, he never snapped like that. "Why?" he now asks himself.

To Greg, he never saw the point of that kind of revenge. Splayed bodies are certainly strewn everywhere, and bewildered survivors are left to clear away the carnage, struggle with the remorse, while this kind of assassin, unloved and unmourned, lies pitiless in a pool of his own blood. What is the point of that?

70

Years pass, the world as a whole tends to forget and move on, and whatever temporary satisfaction might have been derived is eventually overwhelmed.

Violence has never been his way. It is too permanent and ugly, he reasons, with few or no heroes, and far too many victims. Whatever message might have remained is usually lost in the grim aftermath.

He has a more positive and long-term revenge planned, one that may endure long after those immediately at the scene are gone.

Chapter Twenty-one

Especially in the early 1950's, this pristine wilderness that soon enough was built up into the various U.S. Air Force Academy structures, traditions, and facilities must have been incredibly beautiful, vitally untouched as it was back then. So much is pristine still, and virtually unoffending, as it nestles into the wide landscape as Greg exits the freeway.

The several Academy roads are meticulously paved, the shoulders perfectly manicured. Pines and shrubs and thick, wild brush loiter everywhere, unmoved and undisturbed these many years.

The hills here roll massively upward at a slow grade until, finally, Rampart Range rides straight up to the sky. One can almost hear the ancient, volcanic eruptions that pushed these heights up through the Earth's crust to where they now reside, triumphant.

Yet the stillness of an airless moon envelops this entire locale. Dark clouds can mass silently behind this protective range of mountains until the heady gray formations push themselves up over the tops of the various peaks; and a thunderstorm, fully unfurled, rages on an otherwise peaceable summer's afternoon.

Nature is allowed far greater leeway here. Headlights that are flashed during the day at oncoming cars are intended to warn of deer docilely gathered ahead, for wildlife is fully protected here.

No matter the phantom pain that Greg still feels, as if from a severed limb, he has always loved this place. Arriving as he has before too many unknowing tourists invade for the day, he turns the hood of his car toward the Overlooks.

From this remarkable vantage point, the several athletic fields that spread out below currently lie fallow in their off-season. Graduation having occurred several days earlier, the doolies, the new Academy freshmen, are not due to arrive for a few more days yet. A number of cadets are still in residence, however, in numerous summer programs.

Many on the staff are also here, Greg knows from his own experience; but they are on a less stringent schedule than during the academic year.

Parking his Accord, he carefully retraces the concrete steps to the walkway that nearly edges the foliage-encrusted cliffs, cliffs that lead steeply downward to the dirt jogging trail far below.

"I feel as if I'm still running there," Greg once wrote in a poignant paean to this place in the years immediately after his forced resignation when he was still attempting to cope with the bitter loss.

Ironically, it was on this same cement path where the cadet made his first revelations that lead to Greg's betrayal and resignation.

He glances skyward now and locates instead an accommodating raptor, arcing wide in the endless blue above. Soon, he finds himself hitching a joyful ride in these nearby heavens, finally flying high on featured wings.

Far above himself now and his sober past, the lowly Overlooks and the vast Academy grounds, he achieves as perfect a release as anyone might wish for. This, for him, becomes an escape that others can never quite realize in this life.

He quickly finds himself looking down at the old world in an entirely new way, functionally feathered from wing tip to tip, contoured from tail to beak. Fluttering, then soaring high, and gliding so lightly above it all.

Man, he now knows firsthand, only approximates flight, isolated, and fully pressurized, as he must be to survive in the rarified air. Higher, farther, and faster, certainly, yet no better off than this, humans too often achieve significantly less in their tentative endeavors.

Finally, he pulls himself out of this reverie, and his host departs; for he senses that this falcon cannot cry, and he feels a glorious tear of contentment coming on.

Aloft, he remembered those two former cadets: Tom and Donn. One was a friend at Minot, the other an English student of his here. Each was killed in a tragic plane crash, at the point where earth and sky fatally meet.

73

Small metal nameplates on two of the numerous plaques across the way memorialize them in the shadow of the towering Cadet Chapel.

Flight has always had this lethal potential, Greg acutely senses, for all of its winged creatures, of steadily sustaining, or suddenly abandoning, them aloft. Chicks can so cruelly topple much too soon or too often from the comforting nest.

But it is not for these two that he will perform today's mission.

Two other cadets he knew here, two who later died of AIDS, are primarily in his thoughts now as gets back into his car. One was forced out of the Air Force on the eve of graduation for being gay, a promising military career sadly terminated. The other was medically discharged a few years later, a successful flight career ended much too soon.

For Dan and George, and for others he does not even know yet, he will do these things.

Chapter Twenty-two

The sound his Timberlands make along the marbled hallway is more like a soft squish. He knows exactly where to look for the office because some things never change in this mountain fortress.

His unobserved elevator ride to the third floor becomes a cinch, for he quickly learns that he can mask his presence from others. They simply give no thought to his presence, seeing only what they would otherwise have seen if he were not standing there before them. This effort almost becomes like a cheap parlor trick.

He soon finds the plastic plaque on the wall outside the office door: "Office of Special Investigations." He also senses that the OSI secretary is out for lunch.

The single agent is at his desk, preoccupied with paperwork. He cannot hear Greg enter, cannot see him standing nearby and sifting through his brain like sand for buried treasure.

Soon enough, compelled by what motivation he knows not, the agent gets up from his desk, walks to the file cabinets, and unlocks them. To the thoughtless shredder go pages and pages of evidence, documentation, sworn testimony, innuendo, names, dates, alleged incidents. All of them are the only copies currently in existence. Every bit and piece and shred relating to investigations of gay cadets and officers at the Air Force Academy disappear, forever.

Gone irretrievably in an instant are months of work, gathered by typical OSI hook, crook, and skullduggery. But not before Greg writes down the names and flights or departments of both the betrayers and the betrayed, most entirely unaware, as he was 15 years earlier, that they have been identified and are being closely watched.

"Don't ask; don't tell; don't pursue" has been a mockery of justice and hope for gays in the military, Greg knows all too well. He knows what the elected President promised all along, what that President intended to deliver after taking office; and he also knows what cowardly knaves such as Nunn and Dole did to circumvent gay and lesbian civil rights and civil liberties.

He also knows that the Academy strives to blot out any attempt to sully its reputation. Bad publicity is the bane of this highly selective service school. What he has had its own agent do is to ensure that its unsullied reputation is maintained: "I will not lie, cheat, or steal, nor tolerate among us those who do."

Greg's work here done, he reaches outward with his thoughts and carefully bids the agent to sit down again after relocking the secure cabinets, but only after all of their precious information has fled, like the horse before the barn door is lately closed.

On his stealthy way out, Greg grins quite like Alice's Cheshire cat, for this agent, he discovers, is a hopeless homophobe. If ever the finger of blame is pointed toward anyone, Greg realizes, it can only find its way to this evil man, seated here and entirely unaware of what he has been made to do. Yet who else had access to the precious keys?

The smile of satisfaction continues as Greg heads across the Terrazzo level, first to Sijan Hall, named for the Academy graduate who died in a North Vietnamese prison camp, stubbornly refusing to remain in captivity though he was badly injured when shot down and repeatedly beaten after he was captured. At one point, he tried crawling out of the prison camp to escape because his legs were useless. Posthumously, he was awarded the Medal of Honor.

Greg heads up stairwells that he senses to be unoccupied. He merely has to stop twice to blend in with the surroundings once he heads down a dorm hallway since an unauthorized visitor has to be noticed to be reported. At one point, he takes on the appearance of a cadet in a nearby room when three others pass him along a corridor; and he nods familiarly at them as they walk by.

Eventually, he enters the correct room and closes the door.

The brown-haired, husky cadet at the desk looks up, surprised but not alarmed by this sudden intrusion, "May I help you?"

"No, actually," Greg tells him in a low voice, "I'm here to help you, Bill."

Sitting down in the proffered chair, he begins his explanation, "Your roommate suspects that you're gay. He goes through your personal possessions when you aren't here. Some of what he finds he passes along to the OSI. All of this, as you well know, is against

76

Academy regulations; but he and they do not care, as long as he finds effective evidence against you."

The young man's jaw drops two inches, at least.

"Don't worry," Greg assures him, "I've seen to it that all OSI evidence has been surreptitiously destroyed. Don't ask me how; just don't provide them with any more evidence. No matter what they may tell you at a later date, believe none of what they say. They are terrible liars. 'Don't ask; don't tell.'" Greg grimly smiles at the irony of that admonition.

Stunned, nearly beyond belief, the cadet begins to formulate several questions, but Greg stops him, "I understand your concerns and questions, but I just don't have time right now. If any other problems arise, or if you hear about any other gay cadets who may be in trouble, here's my number."

Greg hands him the new, unlisted phone number that he got from the phone company earlier in the day.

He then stands up and moves to the door, "Oh, yeah. I forgot. The black-haired cadet from 11th Squadron that you find so attractive?"

The cadet blankly nods.

"He's gay and thinks you're hot," Greg warmly smiles. "You might ask him to go out on a date. I'm sure he'll accept."

Standing in the open doorway and noting that no one else is nearby, Greg performs his disappearing act by momentarily diverting the cadet's attention. Bill blinks.

"I'm still here," Greg assures him, reappearing. "I just wanted you to realize how I can move about unnoticed. One more thing. If you ever do need help when you call, use the code phrase 'Rainbow Arc of Fire' so I'll know. Good-bye."

The cadet waves; then, embarrassed, he puts his arm down since Greg has departed for good.

The piece of paper with the phone number slips from the cadet's bewildered fingers and drops to the desk. He looks at it again to assure himself that what he has just experienced really happened.

He would not have believed any of it, even with the piece of paper, had the visitor not known that he is gay. He has never admitted that significant fact to anyone before, not even to his family. All of this must have been real, he tells himself. But how?

Chapter Twenty-three

It is like that all over the dorm complexes this day. Several cadets are left bewildered but utterly convinced that they are being forewarned. Greg even visits a few of those malignant cadets who have been their betrayers, leaving most in a profound state of remorse. One, however, proves particularly recalcitrant until Greg spies a recent *Time* magazine on the desk, the issue with winged and heavenly entities on the cover.

"Who the hell are you anyway?" the cadet angrily demands.

"*I am your guardian angel,*" Greg intones in a deep, meaningful and telepathic, voice, planting in the mind of the cadet a vision of celestial light, glowing all about Greg's modest form.

"*You are heading for serious trouble if you continue to perpetrate this evil upon God's gay and lesbian children. They are special ones, and you will reap the whirlwind if you persist in tormenting them. I will certainly not be able to help you then.*"

The young man is stopped, speechless.

He is even more flustered when the "angel" appears to vanish in a flood of white light up and out the open dorm window.

Greg actually dispatched this image while he himself merely walked out of the room in search of his next wayward cadet.

Later, walking near the long, concrete parade strip between Mitchell Hall, the massive cadet dining facility, and Sijan Hall, Greg recalls that visitors used to be able to see dozens of sparkling fountains, years before, that would shoot up geysers of spray in the warm, clear months of spring and summer.

Greg has seen color slides of this spot and those unfettered fountains, their pure stretches of bright aqua blue pools that reflected the wide sky and its cloudy cousins above. Then a concern for water conservation took hold and all of the fountains were filled in with soil and grass.

Now, as Greg traverses from Vandenberg Hall, the other cadet dorm, to the Academic building for one final confrontation, he

79

sees that a few fountains have only recently been restored at either end of the peaceful grove of trees.

He pauses to admire this display of clear liquid made beautiful under pressure. Water soothes and inspires him as no other natural force or substance. It has no mind, no conscience, if you will; but Greg, in his newest sensitivity, determines that it does have a spiritual drive, an energy, as do the trees, the soil, and the grass. A divine purpose is revealed in water that allows it to mix with living substances and make miracles.

Life itself was once sprung from a rich combination of lifeless compounds; water being the catalytic substance and lightening possibly the spark. Yet water, most fluid, can, with other components, become most durable, immovable like concrete.

To know its true essence and to exist according to that light, exclusively, is the genius of water. Greg revels now in the chemistry that allows some of the active molecules to liberate and escape into the atmosphere, while the rest, in a mass, fall under gravity's greater spell and tumble back into the rippling aqua pools. This isn't a clash of opposing wills here in this agreeable fountain. It is a harmonious rearrangement of elements, each a component in a grander scheme that mankind has been allowed to fashion and observe.

Quantity is never reason enough for immobility or for the use of force, even if water is the most extensive medium on the planet's surface, in the shifting shape of the seas. Even the seven great oceans, for all of their bulk and bluster, are continuously moved about by the moon above, Greg recalls. A few billions of years from now, the sun for all its current potency will boil away all of these precious fluids, and life will have had its run here.

Though some humans should escape, what will they have taken, and what will still reside, when even the sun has cooled sufficiently and withdrawn fully from our molten rock?

Chapter Twenty-four

Fairchild Hall, the academic building, brings back the most notable memories, especially the top floor where the instructor and department offices are located. Greg has difficulty maintaining his cover with so many conflicting emotions of his own to control while trying to cloak himself from others.

He recalls how, during the first few days after he arrived in the summer of 1978, he was uncharacteristically lost in this maze of cubicles and corridors, making his way back and forth between the English Department and the elevator that leads one down to the staff cafeteria and to the parking garage below. Riding up alone in the main east elevator this afternoon, he cannot forget his final day here. While he was removing all of his personal belongings and books, the elevator became stuck between floors, so that, symbolically, even the building sensed the wrong in letting him go. Greg chose, even then, not to see the elevator incident as a mere coincidence.

Now standing where his old supervisor's office was, two cubicles in from his own, he can gaze out of the wide, tinted windows and look down at the parade field below, and then beyond to the Black Forest in the distance, across the Interstate.

"How could they be allowed to see so far, stand so high above, and yet be so little aware of what others are made to suffer?" he wonders.

Lost in the past, he does not hear the soft footsteps on the carpet behind.

"May I help you?" the distantly familiar voice asks.

Greg turns around, startled, and immediately recognizes a face from years ago, older now but still familiar. Before another thought can pass, Greg diverts the other man's attention.

As Greg quietly slips away unnoticed, the other is bewildered, imagining that he must be seeing things, with only the gray, inexplicable glass before him.

"Let him believe that his department is haunted," Greg determines, ruefully. He had always liked the head of the English

Department, Colonel Worthy; but then his was the form rejection letter that Greg received a year before, turning him away from the civilian staff position that he knows now he was eminently qualified for.

The Colonel simply did not want to deal with any potential controversy. At least Greg now has the satisfaction of knowing that he was, indeed, the best-qualified candidate for the assignment. He was rejected once again, however, because he is gay.

Intensely angry now and agitated as those past rejections well up, he has devised the most ruthless and, many might even say, blasphemous guise he can come up with. Walking down the hallway and entering the offending Major's office in a blaze of light, Greg approaches as to a mighty vengeance. Yet his entire demeanor is restrained, beatific, and especially saddened, dealing as he must with a misguided and lost sheep, strayed ever so far from the righteous flock.

The terrified, trembling man immediately falls to his knees, shocked that the one vision that he has so often prayed for is now defiantly arrayed before him. He is even more stunned with the admonition that his Redeemer lays out for him, pointing at the extreme error of his ways in using sacred text to taunt and torment innocent others.

As the luminosity painfully dims, the man is left alone on the floor with his lonely conscience, quite overwhelmed with intense remorse.

Greg quickly flees, feeling embarrassed at what his powers have wrought, how he has used them to cheap effect. The end is achieved, but the means seemed far too extreme, even against one who has ruined, was attempting still to ruin, the careers of several of his trusting colleagues.

Chapter Twenty-five

Before he leaves the Academy, Greg walks back across the Terrazzo to the one place that he never fails to visit: the memorial level beside the Academy Chapel. Descending the concrete steps, he moves along the lower walkway, eyeing one plaque after another. So many names, so many lives are accounted for here. He reaches the neighboring pair of plaques where Donn and Tom are separately listed.

Has it really been 11 and 10 years, respectively? He listens for the sound of the pine trees shuffling themselves on the slopes above the chapel, certain that the great memorial tuning fork erected high up there should find their benevolent spirits focused to speak to him. Regretfully, profound silence is all that he hears.

From this spot, just for reassurance, he walks into the Catholic church around the corner. No one is present but himself. The altar is awash in white. He speaks softly, "I neither believe nor disbelieve, as you know. As you also know, I never mean disrespect." He repeats this same benediction in the Synagogue nearby before moving on.

Above, in the Protestant Chapel, he stands transfixed for several moments, staring upward at the colorfully illuminated windows, suffusing everything about him with a pastel glow. The single candle burns nearby and does not flicker. Never before has he realized that the refracted beams filtering through the stained glass make of themselves a rainbow up and down the interior spines of this enclosed space. The immense, hovering cross soars high above the altar as if on limbs outstretched. One can, only with some slight difficulty, see the thin support wires that firmly hold it in place.

While he stands in reverent solitude, he garners no sense of admonition for the course that he has thus far taken. Perhaps it is only his imagination when he again feels that familiar tingling, the same sensation that he experienced so recently on his mountain retreat.

A final stop at the Visitor's Center is required, to pay his respects to its namesake, Barry Goldwater, whose portrait hangs near the entrance. Ever since his heroic and forthright editorial written a year earlier in defense of the President's initial policy on gays in the military, Greg has maintained a new devotion to the man about whom it was said, "In your heart, you know he's right."

"Indeed I do," Greg smiles.

On his way out, he buys two souvenirs, in deference to his having won the lottery: a pair of plaid Air Force athletic shorts, and a carved, painted, wooden display model of a MATS, four-engine, C-124 Globemaster. A propeller-driven, cargo transport from a bygone era, it is a majestic aircraft that he walked through as a kid with his dad in the mid-'50's, at an air show at March Air Force Base in Southern California. He can trace his desire to join the Air Force back to that experience.

He makes one final stop in Colorado Springs, at a particular auto dealership, owned by a well known, if terribly misguided and intolerant, Christian gentleman. He is one who has created many difficult days and nights for gays and lesbians in Colorado and elsewhere since the mean-spirited amendment that he sponsored was passed by foolish, prejudiced, mislead, or ignorant voters across the state. Even though his amendment is currently tied up in the courts, kept at bay for now from enactment, the stubborn man needs to be taught the supreme error of his ways.

Thinking about the encounter later on the freeway, Greg feels certain that he got the deep Voice right; however, the convenient, potted rubber plant, burning yet unconsumed, lacked a certain look of authenticity that he'd hoped for. Still, he knows that he's left one more bigot decidedly less sure of his convictions than he once had been.

Chapter Twenty-six

On his way back to Denver, he is finally forced to deal with certain difficult drivers. "If I don't intervene, who will?" he reasons. He grants that speed limits can be a nuisance, but some people seem to have forgotten that *some* sort of limit is required for everything, especially on the highway.

Most respond rather readily to Greg's surreptitious suggestions that they slow down and be more courteous toward those around them. He converses with them as if he is the other voice that we sometimes hear within our heads when we have a benign discussion within over some random issue or other.

Unfortunately, some drivers demand stern reprimands.

Moreover, a stubborn few require the vision of a State Patrol cruiser in their mirrors to get them to slow down and drive more safely and courteously.

One, in particular, giving the finger when Greg honks at his obstinacy, finds himself breaking his own offending digit against the car door as he attempts to retract it and speed off.

"I guess that lesson will stay with him a while longer," Greg smirks, sorry that a few difficult drivers require stronger measures to persuade them to peacefully coexist with others.

By the time he reaches Denver, all of the drivers around him are now deferential and contented. Once you aim at the ringleaders of bad drivers and reign them in, Greg discovers, the others are happy to stay comfortably within the rules. He doesn't even force them to remain at 65 or 55 mph, the respective speed limits. But he does not allow them to greatly exceed 75 or 65 mph, respectively, even if it does make him feel a bit self-righteous in the process.

He also does not tolerate bullying. Even those in pickup trucks begin using their blinkers routinely. And when they do need to change lanes, they signal their intentions and are surprised to see that other drivers fall back to kindly let them in. Driving is not a competitive endeavor, Greg explains, but a cooperative one.

Only a year before, the same, white, late-model compact car used to speed past him most mornings on I-25, heading north, dangerously dodging in and out of traffic. Greg would shake his head at the reckless predictability of this motorist's daily behavior. This had almost become a tiresome joke to him until, one morning, he saw that same car, wedged underneath a semi. The morning paper the next day confirmed that the husband, who was driving, and his wife, seated on the passenger's side, had not survived the impact. The only reason their work companion in the back seat lived was because she had been lying down, napping, at the moment of the crash.

Now vividly recalling that horrific experience, he thinks to himself, "I guess some people have to be saved from themselves."

With that thought in mind, he looks about at the other drivers around him and realizes that this is a kind of conformity we can all live with, noting that he hasn't enjoyed such a pleasant time behind the wheel in a long, long time.

"We should do this more often," he vows.

Chapter Twenty-seven

He brought his gym bag with him, and so he takes Colorado Boulevard north to his fitness center, correcting only a few more negligent drivers en route.

In the locker room, he eyes himself in one of the many mirrors. For someone who will turn 45 in late September, the same day that Bruce Springsteen also turns 45, he looks fit. His medium brown hair has a significant number of distinguished gray strands along the sides; but overall, it isn't thinning too noticeably. "Well, maybe a little in front," he is forced to admit.

He's always taken care of himself, recently winning a gold medal in the Colorado State Games this spring in men's double's badminton, a sport he played avidly in college and in the Air Force, named Officer-in-Charge of the Academy team in 1979.

He is surprised to notice, however, that his large T-shirt, Don't Panic's "It's Not Just a Phase," fits him a bit more snugly in the shoulders, chest, and sleeves. He's been using free weights for the past seven months; that must be the answer.

In the weight room, he puts his usual, single 45-lb plates on either end of the bar and lies prone on the bench. He pushes the bar upwards, yet finds these ten repetitions surprisingly effortless. He puts the bar back onto the supports and then stands up, puzzled. He adds another 45-lb weight on each end and lies on the bench again.

This weight is also too light, and now he knows something has changed. He adds a third 45-lb plate to each end and tries yet another ten reps. This, too, is accomplished with no significant strain.

He has to borrow two additional 45-lb weights from the adjacent weight rack. By now, though, his quiet efforts have drawn the subtle attention of several other weight lifters.

"Want a spot?" the guy next to him asks, awed in spite of his attempt to appear only mildly impressed.

He'd rather not have witnesses to this personal experiment; but to be polite, Greg tells him, "Sure."

This time, although he knows that he could probably add yet another 45-lb weight to each end and be only moderately challenged, he pretends to struggle just a bit with the last repetition.

"Good job," the other guy tells him, straining to guide the heavily weighted bar back onto the twin supports.

"Thanks," Greg replies, getting up. Then he sees himself again in the full-wall mirror immediately behind the row of benches and does a double take. He is remarkably bigger, so much so that even he now notices it.

Strolling out of the weight room as casually as he is able, he immediately heads for the scales, hoping that no one is watching.

There, he blanches. While never before has he weighed any higher than 168, he now weighs 188.

"That means I'm about 185 if you discount the weight of my gym clothes and shoes!" Greg realizes, backing off of the electronic scale and almost stumbling.

Moving to several of the machines in the main exercise room, he discovers that his strength has correspondingly increased on all of them. Not only do the strength exercises show marked improvement, so do the endurance exercises like leg lifts and reverse sit-ups.

Embarrassed, not only because several of the guys are eyeing him admiringly, but a few of the women are as well, he flees back into the locker room. Finding that only a couple of self-absorbed gym rats are there, he unlocks his locker, tosses in his gym clothes, gets out a towel, and tries to casually saunter toward the showers, unobserved. He cannot avoid looking in the omnipresent mirrors, however, and sees a stunning physical presence.

He stops and stares at his remarkable new reflection. "If I didn't know it was me, I'd ask myself for a date," he mumbles, dumbfounded, and then he ducks into the shower room before anyone sees him.

The warm water trickles down his sturdy back and thick legs, and he tries to contemplate this latest development. "I could wash a load of clothes on this stomach," he laughs, feeling the ripples.

He quickly dries himself. Then he heads to the sinks to shave off the stubble that was part of his disguise at Lottery Headquarters. Soon, he walks back to his locker.

As he is dressing, an incredibly handsome man in his early 30's, the kind one usually sees on the cover of fashion magazines like *GQ*, a man whom Greg has admired for a several weeks, walks past.

Greg catches him looking back. "How are you doing?" the Greek God casually asks; but Greg knows a come-on when he hears one, even as his jaw drops at this unexpected interest.

Unsteady, he replies, "I'm fine. How are you?"

"Great," the guy tells him, heading for the showers. "Will you still be here when I finish?"

"I'm sure I'll still be here," Greg responds, completely unnerved.

"Good. I'd like to ask you to dinner," he smiles warmly.

"Fine."

After he walks off, Greg runs a quick check and realizes that the guy has had some interest in him all along. He doesn't have any idea that Greg has won the lottery since the evening news broadcasts haven't reported his winning yet, and the papers won't run their articles until the morning editions. His interest is legitimate, in Greg as he has always been and not because of what he's only recently become. "I'm surprised."

When the guy returns and towels off, he offers his hand, "My name's Lance."

"I'm sure," Greg thinks, stopping himself from looking down. "Mine's Greg."

"So, are you free this evening for dinner?" he coolly ventures.

"I have no plans at the moment."

"Wonderful. I'd like you to be my guest."

"I'd be delighted," Greg calmly says; but what he's actually thinking is, "I'll be your slave."

Chapter Twenty-eight

Lance follows Greg to his apartment so that he can park his car, feed his cats, and change for dinner.

Inside the apartment, Greg turns on the stereo for Lance while he ducks down the hallway to the back bedroom, feverishly trying to decide what to wear. Sneezer and Schnozz, sitting on the carpet in the living room, side-by-side like stern judges at a kangaroo court, eye the intruder warily. Sneezer soon yawns and sidles off down the hallway. Schnozz hops effortlessly onto the arm of the Southwestern sofa and curls up. Neither acts impressed with Lance.

He is soon up off the couch, strolling around the living room, looking at the Impressionist prints on the back, and side, walls. Then he picks up one of the die-cast Franklin Mint 1950's-era automobiles on the large glass and chrome display shelf to examine it. Finally, he twirls one of the propellers of the carved, wooden TWA Super G Constellation display model that Greg purchased at the Smithsonian Air and Space Museum on a recent vacation back East to visit Roger and Joe, two friends in Virginia.

Lance's moves are studied, graceful, in full command of his lithe anatomy as if he were modeling expensive clothing on a fashion designer's runway in Paris.

Meanwhile, in the bedroom, Greg is just about ready; however, he still does not understand why someone like Lance, the epitome of urban sophistication, would be the slightest bit attracted. His wardrobe looks eminently tailored, his body sculpted.

As Greg hesitates, sitting on the bed next to Sneezer and petting his soft fur, he shakes his head in puzzlement. He does not try to probe for the reasons why, mostly because of what he and Mike discussed the evening before.

His own family is lower middle class. He has always defined his looks as in the middle third, perhaps a bit on the lower end of that middle third. "Oh, well," he tells himself, standing up.

Striding into the living room with as much confidence as he can muster, Greg announces, "I'm ready."

"I love this Manet," Lance tells him, referring to the great artist's masterpiece, *A Bar at the Folies-Bergere*, hanging on the back wall.

"Thanks," Greg replies, pleased that Lance knows and appreciates fine art, even if this is only an expensively framed print. "It's one of my favorites."

"Shall we go?" Lance asks.

"Sure."

He is relieved to discover that Lance has selected *Bistro 100*, a neither pricey nor snobbish art deco restaurant next to Garbo's on 9th Street and Lincoln.

Greg has never been one to feel comfortable in stuffy, high class, pretentious restaurants with snooty maitre d's, menus he cannot fathom, and prices he cannot afford, his current lottery winnings notwithstanding.

Lance parks his gorgeous new jet-black BMW on Sherman Street, having made their reservations on his car phone. Greg admires the fine leather seats as the two of them get out and stroll toward the restaurant in the warm evening air.

"Tell me a little about yourself," Lance casually asks.

"Well," Greg begins, knowing that this ritual is a necessary part of meeting someone new, "I was born in Florida in 1949, raised in California, and I've lived for the past 16 years in Colorado. I'm a contract technical writer at BMI, north of Boulder, and I still have a home in Colorado Springs that I rent out since I started working at BMI three years ago."

"I always thought you looked like a teacher," Lance offers.

"I have been," Greg chuckles. "I first taught at the Air Force Academy. Then, I taught part-time evening classes at Fort Carson and Peterson Air Force Base for years."

"What did you teach?"

"Everything: Humanities, history, literature, English, political science, communications."

"My, that's quite a résumé. Why aren't you teaching now?"

"No full-time openings ever came my way. I even have a secondary-education certification in English, but I only had three

91

interviews after I got my certification. Besides, the job I do now pays well."

"So you're telling me that you sold out?" Lance laughs.

"Yes," Greg grins. "I did."

Sitting in a comfortable booth in the northeast corner of the elevated dining area, Greg asks, "How about you? I've seen you at the gym for a few weeks now, but I know nothing about you."

Lance smiles warmly and begins, "I'm an investment broker. Graduated from CU Boulder. I was born in Colorado and have lived here most of my life. I tried California for a few years but never quite fit in, so I came back here. My family still lives in Boulder, actually."

"Do your parents know?" Greg asks.

"That I'm gay?" Lance replies, immediately aware of what the question refers to. "Yes. My mother accepts it; it was a bit more difficult for my dad."

"It usually is, for dads. Mine had a problem, too. I'm really not sure why that is."

"Maybe they're disappointed that you won't be carrying on the family name. Something like that," Lance offers.

"You're probably right. Reproduction typically is so heterosexual that I have trouble with the concept. I'm not very good at thinking like a straight person."

"Did you date women in college?" Lance asks.

"Me?" Greg smiles, surprised at the question. "Hardly ever."

"Ever been with a woman?" Lance grins.

"You mean sexually?" Greg responds, eyes widening in disbelief.

"Yes, sexually," Lance confirms, still grinning.

"No. Never," Greg laughs, looking around and then lowering his voice. "That would be disgusting and unnatural. Yuck! How about you?"

Lance laughs heartily, "No. Never had any interest."

"I agree. God made gay men to be with gay men; lesbians to be with lesbians; and straight people to be with one another, raising children in the suburbs, taking out life insurance policies, and dying at an early age of heart failure."

"You have an amusing way of putting things," Lance smiles.

92

"Thanks."

Greg decides to make a confession, "I have to tell you something."

"You do?" Lance asks, suddenly wary.

"I just won the Colorado lottery."

"Really?"

"Yeah. I didn't want you to hear it from anyone on the street or read about it in the newspaper. I feel so ashamed," adds Greg, eyes downcast in mock humiliation.

"How much did you win?" Lance inquires, feigning disgust.

"The first check was over $250,000. I wasn't sure that you'd still want to go out with me once you knew the truth."

"I'm glad you told me," Lance says quietly. "I wouldn't want a potential relationship to begin with any secrets between us."

This comment, even if intended humorously, starts Greg's conscience churning. How would Lance react if he knew that Greg can read minds?

"I have to tell him," Greg determines, regretfully. "But I'll wait until *after* dinner."

Chapter Twenty-nine

After a marvelous meal, Lance suggests that they have a drink next door at Garbo's. Greg readily agrees, encouraged that their evening together is continuing and figuring that the bar is as good a place as any to tell Lance the whole truth and nothing but the truth.

Inside, Lance selects, ironically, the very table on the lower level where Greg met the pagans on Friday night and thus began his personal odyssey.

"Can it only have been three nights ago?" Greg asks himself, shaking his head.

"So much has happened in such a short time," he thinks, sitting down uneasily, not at all certain that telling Lance everything will be good for a budding relationship. He has rarely had such a wonderful time on a first date, and he hasn't even felt the need to use his newfound abilities. But he realizes that he might as well learn right away whether or not Lance can handle a potential lover who can read his mind because his attitude on that probably won't change, even over time. Greg doesn't figure that it's something one can get used to, like the fit of a new pair of shoes.

After Lance orders a glass of white wine for himself and a Calistoga for Greg, Greg clears his throat, "I'm enjoying myself immensely, Lance."

"Me, too," Lance readily agrees, sipping his wine.

"Besides winning the lottery," Greg reveals, "something else rather extraordinary happened to me over the weekend."

"More extraordinary than winning the lottery?" Lance asks, unconvinced, setting down his glass. "It would have to be something quite unusual."

"Oh it is," Greg confesses, lowering his voice. "In fact, it all started at this very table, last Friday night."

"Really?"

Greg launches into a description of the mountain trip, the various ceremonies he witnessed, the changes that have taken place to him, and even about the journey to the Academy earlier in the day.

Increasingly, Lance has looked skeptical, and then visibly uncomfortable.

"Have you sought professional help?" he finally asks Greg, his tone becoming most uneasy as he looks about, glad that no one else is sitting on the lower level who can overhear these bizarre revelations.

"You don't understand," Greg tries to explain. "I'm telling you the truth, as weird as this story sounds."

"Right," Lance says, apparently confused as to what course to take next. "Perhaps we both need some fresh air?" He starts to get up.

"*Sit down!*" Greg mentally commands.

Lance stares at Greg's mouth, dumbfounded. "You spoke to me but your lips didn't move." He drops back down into his seat.

Greg continues to communicate telepathically, "*I wanted to tell you the truth because you did mention that we should* not *have any secrets between us.*"

"Right," Lance protests in his thoughts, "but I was only joking." He's trying to determine if Greg can read his mind as well as speak telepathically.

"*I have found,*" Greg continues in telepathic reply, "*that people often joke about what they consider important. This is the first time that I have read your mind since you first spoke to me at the gym. Imagine what it's been like. Three days ago, I was a normal, everyday, garden-variety fag. I take a brief excursion into the mountains with some pagans and come back 'with powers and abilities far beyond those of mortal men.' I'm a decent person, a nice guy. I've never been a Superman, but I'm learning how pretty quickly. Necessity is a great teacher.*"

He resumes speaking aloud, "As gays, we're always treated as misfits and outsiders. I was hoping for a little understanding from someone who knows what it's like to be different from what is considered 'normal.'"

"I'm sorry," Lance says, genuinely perplexed. "I asked you to go out with me because I've thought that you were an attractive and even intriguing man. I guess I didn't realize how interesting you are."

95

"Thanks. I think."

"But isn't this a bit much to reveal on a first date?"

"When would have been a good time to tell you this?" Greg pleads. "Second date? First time in bed together?"

"I see your point," Lance flatly states. "I thought that maybe you were going to tell me that you were HIV positive, something like that."

"Well, I'm HIV negative, if you really want to know. I suppose that's more of a typical piece of vital information to discuss on a first date," Greg says, trying not to sound too sarcastic.

"Actually, these days, it is," Lance tells him, looking down at the table, uncomfortable.

Greg does not attempt at this moment to fill the silence.

Lance fingers the stem of his wine glass, distracted, "I guess I was looking for a husband to take out the garbage, read me the comics from the Sunday paper. You tell me, on the other hand, that you can read my most intimate thoughts, even manipulate my behavior and make me see things that aren't there."

He looks at Greg intently, "The mind is often the only private refuge that we have any more, what with computers, electronic surveillance, and psychoanalysis. Heck, my family doesn't even like to answer census surveys because they feel that their privacy is being invaded."

"I understand," Greg informs him. "I wouldn't have told you if I thought that you couldn't handle it. Maybe I was wrong."

"This is going to take some getting used to," Lance reveals. "You said yourself that you're not even sure that you've stopped changing. If this much has happened in three days, what will you be like in a week, a month?"

"I don't know," Greg confesses, feeling the moment slipping away from him. "But nothing that has happened to me so far has been bad. Even my body has gotten larger and stronger."

"Yeah," Lance awkwardly smiles, the first time since this conversation began. "You're going to have to invest in some new, larger shirts." He points to the tight sleeves of Greg's pullover Polo.

"Yes," Greg laughs, looking at his arms. "They're starting to cut off circulation."

96

The next few minutes of conversation go essentially nowhere, Greg realizes.

Lance soon looks at his watch, "I guess we'd better get moving. I have to be up early tomorrow for work."

"Right."

Greg knows that it doesn't matter whether or not Lance is telling the truth. It's over. He's experienced this sort of brush-off too many times.

At the BMW, Greg says, "I'd prefer that you not tell anyone about our conversation tonight. I'd rather that this not get around."

"I understand," Lance admits. "I know that I'm incredibly spooked about it, and I consider myself fairly open-minded about things."

Greg says nothing as he gets into the black sedan, immediately engaging the safety belt out of habit.

Chapter Thirty

Lance pulls up to Greg's apartment building and stops.

"You're welcome to come up for a few minutes if you'd like," Greg offers, certain that Lance will refuse. This, too, is part of the ritual.

"I really need to get home and go to bed," Lance carefully explains, hoping that his true thoughts aren't being explored in detail.

"I understand," Greg nods. "You have my new phone number. You're welcome to call me later in the week if you'd like to go out again. I certainly enjoyed your company tonight."

"Thanks."

"Well," Greg adds, reaching for the door handle, "I better go."

Lance leans over and hugs Greg, giving him a long, passionate kiss.

That ritual concluded, Greg gets out of the car, closes the door, and waves. Lance returns the wave and drives off.

"I wish they wouldn't do that," Greg says to himself, referring to the warm kiss. "I'm sure that he won't call, but it's hard to dislike someone who kisses that sweetly. Oh well, at least he didn't promise that he'd call. They almost never mean it."

He walks forlornly into his building and up to his apartment.

Dropping onto the couch as the cats gather around, he tells them, "Well, kids, dad struck out again. This time it's not because he's ugly or puny or doesn't have a lot of spare cash lying around. This time, it's all because he's got these terrific powers that seem to terrify ordinary people."

Greg feels the need to talk to Mike; he quickly dials the number. "Hey, guy, it's Greg. Have I got a story to tell you?"

He explains all about meeting Lance and their unfortunate date. "I told him about me because I didn't want him to find out on our wedding night that he married a Martian."

"Yeah, I know it isn't funny; but you gotta admit, it's a hoot."

98

"Oh, yeah, by the way, I now have the body of Hercules. Well, not exactly, but pretty close. I can't quite bend steel with my bare hands, though; but weaker metals don't have a chance."

"The other reason I called was to tell you that I'm sending you a check tomorrow for $10,000. Don't argue with me. You're going back to school, and this will pay off that credit card of yours. Besides, it's the legal limit I can give without your having to pay taxes on it."

"Yeah, I know, I'm a frigging saint. Actually, that's one divine figure I haven't portrayed today. Let's see. I was an Angel, then Jesus Christ, and finally God."

He explains about his day at the Academy and Colorado Springs.

"I agree that it serves them right. In retrospect, I don't feel a bit guilty about doing it. They're always using their religious symbols against *us*; I thought they deserved a little of their own spiritual medicine. Besides, I'm convinced that Jesus would give them a good verbal throttling were he ever to have a mind to return."

"OK. I better let you get to sleep. I promised I'd go into work in the morning. In addition, I have to call Barbara in the Springs. You know, my librarian friend? Yes, I always call her each week and we talk about how we didn't win the lottery again. This time, I have a surprise for her. I'll have to give her my other rows of lottery numbers in case they'll be lucky for her."

"Right. Good night, Mike. I love you, too. Take care."

As he places the receiver onto the cradle, he has a strange sensation that someone is up to no good in the alley.

Chapter Thirty-one

He bolts through his apartment door; the cats follow to the sill and stop, wondering what's the matter.

He races down the stairs and out the side door, exiting under the carport. He immediately spies a young man with a can of spray paint, applying a graphic design to a garage door across the alley.

"Hey," Greg yells out, "I don't think the owner would want you to do that."

The young man wheels about, dropping the spray can and pulling a gun from his baggy jeans. Before Greg can react, he fires.

"Shit!" Greg exclaims as he recoils sideways in time for the bullet to barely graze his arm instead of hitting his chest. His new, increased quickness saved him. Still, blood flows from the wound.

Mentally, he orders the kid to drop the gun. Instead, the jerk fires again, Greg ducking in time so that the bullet hits a brick building behind him.

Thinking fast, Greg sends a mental image of himself escaping down the alley. The kid fires at the fleeing figure.

In a moment, Greg is at the kid's side and decks him with one angry fist to the chin.

The kid collapses backward onto the blacktop, the gun falling from his hand.

Greg kicks it aside with his foot and then drops to the ground, the powerful new adrenaline in his system still racing fast.

He eyes the kid keenly, wondering why his command to drop the gun had no effect. Even now, he feels the intense hatred and evil that pervaded the kid's mind.

"The intensity must have blocked my thoughts," he realizes.

Telepathically, he seeks out a nearby police car. He locates one on the other side of Cheesman Park. Subtly, he directs the officer to the alley.

As the cruiser turns the corner, Greg stands up and waves. The kid is still out.

Like a rabid dog or crazed psychopath, the kid was pure malevolence. "I guess that I better be more careful from now on," he tells himself as he provides the officer with a generally truthful account of what happened. He leaves out the part about creating a mental image of himself for the kid to shoot at while he knocked him out.

"Aren't you the guy who just won the lottery?" the officer asks him. "I saw you this evening on TV."

"Yeah," Greg responds, realizing that his meager attempt at disguise obviously didn't work too well. "My lucky day."

"You're fortunate that it wasn't your last day. This kid has been involved in several gang incidents recently, one of the really bad ones. What were you doing out here anyway?"

"Taking out the trash," Greg meekly grins.

"Well, I better put in a call for an ambulance to get you to Emergency. That wound doesn't look too good."

As the officer soon puts the cuffed kid into the back seat, Greg moves over to get a look at his youthful adversary.

"What are you looking at, asshole?"

"Nothing at all," Greg responds, involuntarily backing away.

He wonders how someone so relatively young has learned to hate so much.

"Welcome to the real world," Greg tells himself as he watches the police car drive off.

Chapter Thirty-two

Riding in the darkened ambulance and then sitting in the harsh glare of the Emergency Room of Denver General Hospital, Greg has a lot of time to think about what happened to him in the alley behind his apartment building, a place that he imagined to be relatively safe and reasonably sane. Now, some of his own blood is still there, drying on the pavement.

A total stranger, a kid really, tried to kill him, with no regret or remorse, no apparent convictions one way or the other about life and death, guilt or innocence. Hardened beyond belief. Obviously, only Greg's recent physical changes saved him from being killed or badly wounded, even if the mental changes were what alerted him to the kid's presence, marking turf like a dog lifting its leg and spraying.

The newspapers have been filled in recent months with the fallout of these gang wars in Denver. Most of the victims are the rival gang members themselves. Good riddance. However, a significant number of prominent and anonymous innocents have also been caught in the crossfire. Wrong place, wrong time.

Gangs, tagging, drugs, these and more, all part of a battle over turf, over territory, like the classic gun fights of the fabled Old West, unromanticized. Indelible and inflatable ego wars, fueled now, as then, by disappointments, shattered expectations, greed, poverty, denied advancements, betrayed hopes, and even racism, both real and imagined. The list of causes seems endless and insurmountable. No one is responsible, but everyone is guilty. Even in this hospital Emergency Room, the casualties of this continuous conflict, its ebb and flow, even people like Greg now, show up to be treated and released. The world goes on.

This is a world that Greg never had to confront, nor be confronted by, before. Even when a popular local businessman was gunned down, his wife viciously brutalized, by two men who seemed to fester up out of the gutters and into savage notoriety, in the parking lot next to "Queen" Soopers, five and a half blocks from 10th and

Humboldt Streets, there was nothing Greg could do then but shake his head and hope that justice is served.

Greg's mind is forming quickly and firmly into a single motivation: resolve. He is angry and frustrated, as only a recent victim can be. He now has the means, and he will deal with these gangs. He will also see to the many conditions that have given rise to recent gang prominence. As never before, he can expose and treat both symptom and disease, cause and effect. "Either the gangs will be broken," Greg vows to himself, "or the gangs will break me! I prefer *my* chances."

The hospital staff treats him efficiently, if not entirely hospitably. They have far worse injuries to mend than his, and often in greater numbers. He knows, however, that these are dedicated people, overwhelmed sometimes by conditions under which they work, night after night, year after year, seeing the cases that the news media ignores as well as those that they report. The staff has their own kinds of resolve, and they do their jobs far better than one should expect of human beings.

As the nurse cleans his wound and bandages it, she asks him, "Do you have a ride home?"

"Yeah," he explains, thankful that she shows concern. "I called a friend of mine, and he'll be here shortly. Thanks for asking, though."

"You're welcome," she smiles warmly, then she looks down the glaring corridor past Greg and shakes her head. "Better prepare yourself for the deluge. Here come the media!"

Greg looks up and knows instantly what she means. You cannot win $15 million dollars in the morning, get shot in the evening, and not draw a bit of unwanted public attention. "Damn."

"Tell us, Greg," one reporter hurriedly asks him, the video cam running, microphone in his face, "what happened to you tonight?"

"I got a little scratch on my arm in the alley behind my apartment building. It was nothing. The good people at this hospital tell me that I'll be fine after a good night's sleep."

"We heard," insists another reporter, "that it was a young gang member who shot you, that you could have been killed."

"I suppose so," Greg says, trying to maintain an equilibrium here. "He was tagging a neighbor's garage door when I surprised him. I should have called the police rather than try to confront him myself. It was stupid, and it was my own fault."

Although he tries to establish a tone of modesty, he can see the headlines already being formulated in the reporters' minds: "Lotto Millionaire Gallantly Defends Neighborhood from Ruthless Gangs."

The interviews continue for several more minutes, and Greg cannot alter the perception being created that he's a hero, defending himself bravely and successfully in a senseless and unprovoked attack, something that other people only imagine themselves capable of doing if they are ever provided with a similar opportunity.

Ordinary citizens will shudder that it could have happened to them, and they'll be relieved to learn that Greg not only survived the ordeal but also fought back. The criminal was immediately apprehended.

Greg begins to formulate a plan, capitalizing on this impending public ground swell: typical citizens start imagining themselves as similar heroes, ridding their own neighborhoods as they see the gangs crumble, at last beginning to fall.

When motivated, people can and do act heroically, Greg senses, especially when they feel that they have a better-than-even chance of success. Greg knows that he's the one who can foster their better natures, nurture their imaginations, to take that chance and succeed.

Chapter Thirty-three

After the reporters finally disperse, Greg sees his good friend Ramsey Courter making his way through the departing multitude.

He has known Ramsey for 12 years. His black hair and rugged good looks have made him one of Denver's more eligible and popular gay bachelors, but he's not yet met someone who has been interested long enough to settle down. He holds a black belt in Tae Kwon Do, and for several years now has been attempting to build a railroad from Golden, Colorado, to Blackhawk, the prominent gambling mecca up in the mountains above Denver. He's not a proponent of gambling so much as he simply loves steam trains.

Born in the wrong century, perhaps, he now battles environmentalists, state laws, county commissioners, and city ordinances to get this railroad built, while trying to lasso enough reputable and willing investors. Others may see only the profits to be made, but Ramsey sees the romance of a bygone era, when Man's motion through time and space was at the pace of a well-stoked steam engine, hauling passengers or freight up a smoothly graded right-of-way, through pristine mountain canyons, with rocky streams burbling and eddying swiftly by. The lonesome whistle blows every now and then just to hear itself letting off steam.

"I guess I should have had you with me," Greg says, sheepishly, pointing at his bandaged upper arm. "I could have used some help."

"Seems to me that you did OK, from what I've heard," Ramsey grins at him. "Let's get out of here."

Heading out into the warm Denver night in Ramsey's Chevy S-10 extended cab pickup, Greg tells him, "I've been so busy these past couple of days that I didn't have a chance to call you about winning the lottery."

"Or about your trip up into the mountains with the pagans," Ramsey chides, eyeing him suspiciously. "Camping out under the stars seems to agree with you. You look different. Care to tell me about it, Mr. Muscle?"

105

"Oh, yeah, that," Greg laughs, feeling guilty, knowing that he cannot keep anything from Ramsey. "I've sort of had a few significant changes occur that I meant to tell you about. Beyond the fact that I now seem to be built like a 'brick shithouse,' as you would put it."

"I'd say that's a good way to describe how you look. Steroids don't work that fast, and I know you haven't been working out at the gym that hard to be this big, this quickly."

Greg repeats the story that he's already told Mike and Lance. Since Ramsey is a close friend and he has already observed the profound physical changes, he's readily able to believe just about anything.

Ramsey coolly informs him, "You have never before been the kind who would take on a gunman in an alley single-handedly. I knew that there'd have to be some bizarre explanation."

"Bizarre is the best way to describe these past three days. By the way, you told me that you've gone out with Officer Dean Hammond on a 'ride along' before. Is he working tomorrow night?"

Dean is a Denver police buddy of Ramsey and Greg's.

"I'm sure he is."

"Good. I know that his territory covers the Park Hill area, where so much gunfire has occurred recently. That's as good a place as any to start my little urban experiment. I can certainly use his knowledge and help."

"He'll be glad to give it, especially if you intend to break up the gangs. Dealing with them is one of the more discouraging aspects of being a cop right now in this city."

"I hope to make it quite a bit easier for them from now on."

106

Chapter Thirty-four

Officer Dean Hammond has been on the Denver Police force for more than 10 years and is a man of several profound contradictions. Having the large, granite frame of a power lifter, he displays a quick yet dry wit, and this is belied by his soft blond hair and cherubic face. He's a gay man and, at the same time, a card-carrying conservative Republican and Rush Limbaugh fan. With a gentle disposition and generous to a fault, he good-naturedly takes massive ribbing from his more liberal, Democratic friends over his incongruous politics.

On Tuesday evening in the precinct station, Greg arrives early and unobtrusively taps the minds of many of the policemen and women, as well as the detectives he encounters, for any useful information he can glean about Denver gangs and anti-gang tactics.

Later, in the patrol car, Dean warns him, "I hope you got some sleep. This is a tough shift to handle if you're tired."

"I did go to work this morning, and they thought I was crazy to show up after winning $15 million and getting shot, but I had a few projects to wrap up. Then, I was able to go home early and take a nap," Greg advises him.

"How's your arm?" Dean asks.

"Fine, actually," Greg confesses. "It's almost healed."

"Already?"

"Yeah," Greg says. "It seems to be another side benefit to my miraculous transformations these past couple of days. I heal more quickly."

"So tell me about these mental powers that Ramsey hinted at last night," Dean inquires, a smirk creeping over his face. "Maybe you could develop a magic act: 'The Amazing Gregor': knows nothing; tells all."

"Cute," Greg remarks, giving Dean a narrow look. "I could try to read *your* mind; that would take all of five seconds!"

"Touché," Dean laughs.

Greg relents and explains, "I can read minds. As a consequence, I can also see through someone's eyes whenever I want to. In addition, I find that I can persuade or try to order most people to do what I want, although I typically refrain from the latter. Americans are lousy at taking orders. I try instead to finesse them. I can also make people see things that aren't there, or I can disguise something that is present."

"You'd be a hit at parties," Dean responds. "Of course, if the legal system got hold of you, they'd shut down your magic act pronto, no matter how beneficial your abilities might be."

"You've got that right," Greg sighs. "That's why I have asked the few whom I've told to keep the information to themselves. I have no intention of getting tangled up with judges and lawyers and law courts. I'd be out of business fast."

"Now you're starting to sound like Rush," Dean smiles.

"Please, don't get me started. I have no intention of violating innocent people's civil rights, especially their privacy rights. But I am a private citizen with my own set of rights *and* civic responsibilities, which others seem to have forgotten these days."

"Hit that soap box!" Dean calls out, in the tone of a good backwoods preacher.

"Hey," Greg laughs, "these are the streets we're talking about. I've got my own war wound now. This isn't some fancy mahogany and teak law office or stuffy law school where astute professors and intense legal scholars debate the fine points of the law, while criminals run rampant."

"I hear you, brother."

Greg smiles but proceeds, "I consider myself a new weapon against crime. No legal interpretations have yet been handed down on me, although I can imagine them doing that rather easily and quickly if they found out."

"Sure," Dean reminds him. "They'd merely apply the same laws to you that now affect electronic surveillance. You're just another medium for gathering information without another person being made aware. I'd give the courts five minutes to issue an injunction against you."

"That long?" Greg grins.

108

"Maybe three minutes," Dean smiles.

"Well, as the old cliché goes, 'What they don't know won't hurt them.'"

"I've got just one request," Dean ventures.

"Name it," Greg asks, certain he already knows the answer.

"A boyfriend. Can you find me one?"

"You mean one who won't break your heart?" Greg smiles, ironically.

"You got it."

"That'll take a little longer," Greg says, wistfully looking at the city skyscrapers in the distance. "Sure, I'll find you the right guy after we take care of these gangs. It's a promise."

"OK," Dean acknowledges. "So what's the plan tonight?"

"Cruise through the neighborhood," Greg tells him. "I'll keep my mind open to trouble brewing. When a crime is about to be committed, or is committed, you send in the reinforcements. We'll give the gangs enough of their own ropes to hang themselves."

"If this works, you'll put us out of business."

"No, my big, blue friend. I intend to be like a good hunting dog. I'll point. You pick 'em off. I want no publicity. Besides, some crimes are spontaneous and I can't be everywhere at once."

He pats Dean's shoulder, "There'll always be a need for the police as a visible symbol. I discovered on the highway that just the merest glimpse of a cop car in the vicinity and people behave like you've never seen. You're an important deterrent."

"I always knew we were good for something," Dean smiles. "Well, *My Favorite Martian*, get your antennas up," Dean warns him. "We're there."

"You're right. I'm picking up a few bad vibes already."

Chapter Thirty-five

The police cruiser slowly passes the other vehicle, heading in the opposite direction. Greg is able to disguise their presence from the driver, the sole occupant.

"He's got a gun on the seat, covered by a coat," Greg tells Dean. "He intends to hit a house in the middle of the next block. It's a private vendetta between him and a rival gang leader."

"Where are his buddies?"

"They wanted no part in this, so he's going alone," Greg explains. "He's cocky but not too bright."

Dean slowly turns the cruiser around and they follow closely behind the rusting Chevrolet.

"Am I following too closely?" Dean asks, concerned.

"You're fine. He can't see or hear us. Just be ready to cut him off the moment he begins firing."

Halfway down the block, the other driver slows to a stop. He reaches for the gun under the coat and points it out the car window at the house. Two shots strike the structure harmlessly. The gun falls from his hand, landing on the street.

"Cut him off now!" Greg orders.

Dean hits the lights and siren and screeches to a stop, cutting off the Chevrolet.

The driver panics and shoves open the car door, attempting to flee.

Dean is out of his vehicle, weapon drawn. The gang leader tries to run between two houses to escape but trips and falls heavily to the concrete driveway. Dean is over him immediately.

"Don't move," Dean orders, heavy foot on the man's back.

Another police car, ordered by Dean as backup just before the shooting, pulls up and stops. Both officers jump out. One joins Dean in cuffing the suspect. The other retrieves the weapon the man dropped.

A few minutes later, with the other officers taking the suspect to jail, Dean and Greg continue their patrol.

"OK, so why did he conveniently drop the gun?" Dean asks.

"Simple," Greg explains. "I made him think that it was too hot to hold."

"And I suppose you made him trip on the driveway?"

"No, he did that himself," Greg smiles. "I only blinded him to the kid's tricycle that he stumbled over."

"Why did he shoot at the house? You said that nobody was home."

"I made him think that he saw a light on in the living room and then a shadow on the curtains. He really wanted to kill the other guy. Fooling him was easy because I had him see exactly what he wanted to see."

"Some crafty defense lawyer, if he learned the truth about this, would say that you entrapped his client," Dean pointedly remarks.

"How so?" Greg asks, slightly annoyed.

"Well," Dean explains, playing devil's advocate, "you blinded him to our presence. Then, you made him see what wasn't there. The lawyer would argue that you created a situation that lead to the crime. If the suspect had been aware that we were here and that no one was at home, he would never have shot at the house."

"Ah," Greg argues, "but the important issue is *intent* on the part of the suspect. He had the gun, he was in the neighborhood to commit the crime, and he intended to kill his victim."

"How did you know this?" Dean wryly smiles.

"I read his mind," Greg admits.

"Inadmissible evidence," Dean counters. "That's hearsay."

"Oh, well," responds Greg, shrugging his shoulders. "He discharged a stolen firearm in a residential neighborhood, endangering innocent people, with the intent to commit murder. Even he'll admit that he saw a light on and a shadow in the window. Who's going to say that that wasn't the exact truth?" He looks carefully at Dean.

"'I know no-*thing*,'" Dean remarks, shrugging his shoulders and speaking just like the tubby guard Schultz on *Hogan's Heroes*.

"I thought not," Greg grins. "Oh, by the way, you'd better slow down and call for backup."

"What's up?"

"That's a crack house we just passed, filled with drug dealers, making several transactions," Greg announces.

"We'll need a search warrant," Dean reminds him.

"No, we won't," insists Greg. "Bad blood has been forming among those crooks for a long time over profits and the quality of the drugs they're dealing. You're about to hear the sounds of a violent gun fight erupting in just a few seconds."

"You're sure?"

"Positive."

"I'll call for backup," Dean exhales.

Chapter Thirty-six

Over the next several days and nights, the patterns repeat themselves all over this and the surrounding neighborhoods. First Greg, operating as a point man, fingers for Dean the prime suspects and their potential or actual crimes. Then, he gets out of the way to let the criminals commit themselves and the police make the arrests and file the reports. As the anti-gang and anticrime wave washes through one neighborhood and cleanses it, Greg and his police brigade move on to others. Dean discretely finds a few other officers in other precincts who can carry on the work outside of his immediate jurisdiction, and the effort proceeds.

Some gangs, flattering themselves that while others were broken they can succeed, try to carry out their schemes and also fail, miserably. Citizens, as Greg predicted, become emboldened by the successes that they see around them and join with the police, hand-in-hand, in this surge of purification to retake their own neighborhoods, block by block.

Whereas before there had been hostility or indifference, now one finds confidence and cooperation. Individual gang members, witnessing first-hand the dangers of involvement, fall away. Several of them become informants, realizing that the powers of their former leaders are being broken on all sides.

Again, looking for the right fulcrum upon which to apply the lever of his crusade, Greg finds it repeatedly, building upon a core of humanity that proves far more solid and enduring than even he ever imagined. His own petty prejudices against others also fall away as he sees little but heroism and valor, repeatedly, in those whom his actions have rallied. When people believe that they have a chance to make a difference, to make a change, they act.

Then, to shore up these limited gains, he begins to pick out those within and outside the community who have the money, means, and desire to make improvements in the lives of others. He matches talent and initiative to prospects that already have success built in. Jobs exist, he finds, but people need to feel that work is an honorable alternative, even if the money is less, short-term, than what illegal activities and drug sales might bring.

Greg taps the vast reservoirs of self-worth in the community, stabilizing and then working to expand them. This entire task becomes even more important and rewarding than anything that he has done so far.

People all around are receptive so that only a minute amount of persuasion is required on his part, here and there, to begin to channel back from oblivion and hopelessness those who had nearly given up. Some, he finds, will never make the return trip. No amount of glue will piece them back together. This saddens him intensely, like a medic who finds in combat triage that some casualties cannot be saved and he must move on. Some gang members, like the kid who shot him, are so consumed by hate and evil that they refuse, in effect, any rescue. Defiantly, they go down, swinging at air.

As he slowly moves from the neighborhoods to the streets, he finds that some cannot be helped, do not wish it, even among the innocents there. In the mornings, on the weekend, he ministers secretly to those living under bridges, under cardboard or plastic, and delves within the various souls he finds there. He quickly discovers that humans display several levels of walking upright, not physically but emotionally. Some do not wish to return to the acceptable lives they once led; yet he sees that they receive proper medical care before they return to the streets.

Under the overpass of Speer Boulevard, for example, near the bike path along Cherry Creek, he finds a few refugees, sleeping in oblivion, near the rushing civic waterfall, the one with colorful and mystical figures painted almost as talismans, just across from Metro State College.

But their magic doesn't work down here, with the sound of cars speeding by overhead, their drivers preoccupied. A few, he finds, he can help. Touching his hand to their weathered and scruffy faces, he dives deeply, deeper than can social workers or policemen, or concerned citizens who drop a quarter or dollar into a palm or cup.

Sometimes, he lifts the veil but a little, yet healing light begins rushing into minds and hearts that knew only darkness. This, again, like his mission against the gangs, will take time, he senses.

114

And unlike with the gangs, this is a more lonely vigil, requiring constant ministrations, and not just his own. For these individuals are not threats to the populace. They are but expendable people, shunted aside. Demanding little, they get little notice. For most of them, he starts by leaving nutritious food to begin their day. It's a start.

He also seeks out those in the expensive lofts and condos nearby with the caring and the courage and sends them on their way to assist their neighbors. People, he finds, have the time and, when pressed, the money; they just need a focused direction pointed out for their pent-up energy and civic pride to find outlet. He knows that for most of the needy he can be but a beginning that they and others must complete.

On Sunday afternoon, after days of nearly nonstop work, not as a god of any kind, but as a new man, he determines that he needs to rest. He knows that he cannot neglect himself while working with so many. If one spends too much time rummaging about in the minds of others, Greg finds, one endangers one's own consciousness and identity. Therefore, he hugs his cats good-bye at noon, grabs his volleyball net from the closet, and heads for Cheesman Park. To borrow from his favorite movie, *Field of Dreams*, "If you build it, they will come."

Chapter Thirty-seven

Greg has been coming to Cheesman Park to play volleyball on the weekends for four summers now. Since he is often the first to arrive, and usually in the past had to wait for someone with a net to show up, over the winter, he finally bought "The Net," made by Centerline Sports, a local firm. The Net comes with its own red tote bag, two detachable poles, two plastic base plates for the poles, a net, a nylon line to mark the borders of the court, four nylon support ropes to anchor the net, two of them adjustable, four metal spikes to drive in the support ropes, and a laminated instruction sheet, with drawings of how to set up the whole complicated thing. As a minimum, two people are required for setup. One stubborn person can try if he doesn't mind taking forever and looking ridiculous in the process.

Greg has added a hammer to drive in the metal spikes when the ground is hard, a tin of Band-Aids for inevitable cuts and scrapes, an Ace bandage to wrap ice on a sprained ankle or knee, and two tubes of sun block for hot summer days. He hauls all of this and a jug of water the two blocks to the "Gay Beach," the great expanse of flat lawn by the large tree at the west 9th Street entrance to the Park. This area is just off of the paved road that circles through Cheesman, 1.2 miles long.

A decade and a half before, when he first came to Cheesman Park with the three gay cadets, Bill, George, and Dan—the latter two now dead—the Gay Beach used to be located along the slightly elevated quadrant by the sidewalk at the southeast entrance to the Park. However, a bloodless coup, led by the lesbians a couple of years later, easily routed and dispersed the gay men. Towels and thongs and suntan lotion in hand, this defeated band soon migrated to its current location and have been there ever since, soaking up sun and cruising the other gay men driving by.

On early summer days, there can be quite a traffic jam of cars circling the Park. America could probably dispense with foreign oil imports if those cruising by used bicycles and roller blades exclusively instead of Jeeps, convertibles, and pickup trucks, in an endless procession.

A few of the others have told him that spontaneous, as well as serious, gay volleyball has been played in Cheesman Park for years, beginning as far back as 1972. When Greg first began showing up in 1991, he hadn't played since his days teaching at the Academy, more than a decade earlier, and it showed. He was surprised that the others tolerated his painfully slow relearning process.

His friend Dino, who almost never plays because he cannot abide the snooty attitude of some of the others, refers to them all, derisively, as "The Volleyball Vixens," a not entirely fair assessment of them all, just the bitchy few. The vast majority are nice guys, always fun to be around, whose irreverent demeanor and gentle chiding a casual observer might mistake for viciousness.

Newcomers are welcome, especially if they're pretty (whether or not they can play worth a damn). If not pretty, they're certainly welcome if they can pass the first ball high to the setter, set a nice floater off the net to either spiker and block reasonably well, or at least jam a vicious spike down the other team's collective throat.

This day is, as so many are in Colorado, incomparable. The sky is a flawless, brassy blue from one horizon to another. The sun is warm, a slight breeze cool. Trees everywhere on the periphery are bloated and gaudy in their finest greenery, like heady drag queens coiffured for the night. The grass is thickly unblemished although matted here and there amid the sprinkler heads where games were played the previous Tuesday evening or last weekend.

Dogs and their owners crisscross the vast lawn, and Frisbees hover and sail above like interplanetary visitors. Only a few buildings have the audacity to point themselves over or through the surrounding foliage, so that one can barely tell that one is ensconced within a large city. Jets from Stapleton bank and pass higher overhead. An occasional leather man or lesbian roars by on a loud Harley, but mostly the traffic is continuous and subdued.

Blond Chris is often the second to show up, and he helps put up the net that lures the others. Then Terry, Tom, Kenny, Jack and Matt wander in. Eventually, Bill, Lance (the guy with the white Celica, not the black BMW), Niles, Mike, Mark, Brian, and Lee show

117

up. Sometimes, Glen flies in from Salt Lake City, or Eli drives down from Cheyenne, or Rich arrives after soccer or tennis. Scott and Ken are usually late after roller blading. José and Fernando later still. A few Steves and still more Scotts and a couple of Rogers also play, on occasion.

Those and several more can be seen as random teams form and reform. Some combinations win and stay on; others lose and challenge for the next game. Some play two-man if another net goes up. Or four-man if a third net is required.

This is often the pattern of their weekend existence from mid-spring to mid-autumn. Games are played for the Championship of the World, at the moment, until they end and other games begin, all previous scores and records forgotten. Most of the guys are single. A very few like Dave and Vaughn, not here today, are boyfriends who met elsewhere. A few others like Bill have "volleyball widows" for lovers, guys who infrequently watch but never play.

On the high ground of Cheesman Park is The Pavilion, overlooking all contests and play below, a large but not massive marble temple such as the Greeks might have erected to worship their own deities. A fountain in each of the two pools immediately below The Pavilion shoots a strong spray into the air in the warm months, where dogs and children and playful others cavort and splash around to cool off.

This day on the volleyball court, Greg does not take off his T-shirt, the extra-large "Clinton - Gore '92" campaign banner that has always before been much too baggy. He's become too muscled too quickly for the others not to notice and become suspicious if he weren't sheathed in so much cotton.

Always in the right spot, always with the steady bump or hit, he makes no mistakes, no miss-hits; but no one really notices. All of his serves drop in effortlessly. His spikes he eases up on, his consistent blocks are not always effective. Too improved play too fast would certainly draw suspicion. He won't even use his new mental faculties because he already knows where the others will likely hit the ball or spike it, or dink it over the net when confronted by a block.

118

Even with his increased range and quickness, no one can guard against every effective shot or the misplayed ball that lands true. With his new abilities, he cannot react to all of the mistakes of others or especially to their unpredictability under game conditions. He plays as best he can, given the fact that he doesn't want to reveal that he could wipe the court with every one of them. Winning, in fact, isn't everything here. He enjoys their company and this game more than that.

At one time or another, he was attracted to Kenny, Randy, Roger, and Matt. But it didn't take a mind reader to know that each one was not interested. Although tempted, today he doesn't delve into their reasons why. He does, however, in celebration for having won the lottery, offer to take them all to Racines restaurant for dinner. A few demur, but he insists and they soon agree to go.

Racines is located off of 9th Street, near Speer Boulevard, two blocks west of Broadway. Gay-friendly and sporting a Southwestern decor, the smoking area of this popular eating establishment is usually the most advantageous place to sit if you want to be among other gays. This night, however, Greg has called ahead and reserved the patio for the occasion.

Finally, good food and wine having been freely consumed, and other, generous toasts having been made, Greg rises to propose one of his own: "To all of my buddies gathered here. May we forever play volleyball together in Cheesman Park."

"Here, here," several reply.

Greg vows to himself, as he looks out at the smiling throng, that he will do what he can to find life partners for those who are single and looking, especially for those whom he has found particularly attractive yet who haven't found someone they're attracted to.

"They deserve to be happy," he tells himself.

Chapter Thirty-eight

After dinner at Racines, several of the guys head to *The Foxhole*, the Sunday afternoon and evening summertime bar, out beyond Union Station, across the railroad tracks from where the huge new Coors Field baseball stadium is being built for the Colorado Rockies National League club. The massive stands for baseball fans look directly out from behind home plate right down into *The Foxhole*, whose open-air patio surrounds a massive oak that has stood in place for many years.

Few are optimistic that *The Foxhole* will survive the onslaught of major league baseball into this neighborhood of warehouses and dirt parking lots. It and *Reflex*, the gay Friday and Saturday night dance bar just west across the shared parking lot, that used to be called *Tracks* a decade and more ago, now reside insecurely.

On the other side of the tracks, in the area of Denver known as LoDo, short for Lower Downtown, many sports bars and restaurants have already appeared, in anticipation of opening day. Only time will tell if the two bastions of gay and lesbian weekend partying can endure, especially since Coors Field does not have nearly enough parking spaces in and around its periphery for all of those who will attend the games and won't use public transportation. Had the new 5.3-mile, showcase RTD light rail line been positioned a half-mile farther to the west, more baseball fans could have parked elsewhere and taken the quieter electric cars to the ballpark.

Speculation has it that either *Reflex* or *The Foxhole*, or both, will metamorphose into straight sports bars, or be torn down, spelling doom for gay bars in this part of the city. A tradition that has survived for at least a decade and a half will die.

Greg knows that with all of his powers of concentration, he won't be able to hold back this kind of inevitable change. What AIDS and Amendment 2 couldn't kill, progress and professional sports might, and he cannot stand in the way.

Chapter Thirty-nine

The ritualistic dance music is blaring, inevitably and loudly, into the hot evening air, spilling over the exterior fence and out toward the city skyline where, here and there, some lights are still on in the accumulating skyscrapers. Burgers and dogs grill furiously in the large brick barbecue pit near the open air entrance to the bar, as the dripping fat freely falls into the fire, sending up mass formations of pungent smoke.

Greg purchases several pitchers of beer, handing them out amongst his volleyball mates and sending them on their merry way into the swelling crowd of half-naked revelers, new sunburns and old tan lines in ample evidence here.

It's a good night to be gay and at *The Foxhole*, with its Rainbow and Colorado State flags fluttering loosely above the pointed roof in an ineffectual yet persistent breeze.

Moments in time can be held like this. And a similar string of such events can be linked in one's memory like pearls or precious jewels on a golden thread. A place that friends and familiars go to for years on certain magic summer nights can find its way into a kind of permanence that transcends change or destruction. If the living maintain them in their heads, warmly, the sleeping spirits of the dead dance on, as smiles that are not forgotten.

Greg thinks of Dan and Dick, Neil and Kenny, and Vince and Tom, partners who have died, partners who have since broken up, and partners who still dance together here, uniting us in our revelry and reverie. Greg looks up into the stolid oak, their sturdy overseer, with its many twinkling strands of tiny white lights, an incongruous yet comforting Christmas-like effect in the midst of an opposite season. He wonders now about how many have stood at one time or another under its sheltering branches in years and summer thunderstorms past. Its green leaves are distinctly fewer in number now, as the stout tree ages, as there are fewer leaves in the gay community whose survivors are made somber on several occasions each year by certain passages.

"Yet the shelves are restocked annually," Greg is fond of saying whenever he looks out at the many dancers and the various clusters of conversationalists and realizes that there seem to be as many gay men and lesbians here as there ever were. A community thrives because of shared ritual and bonding. The living and the dead, as well as the dying and those being born, come together historically in places like this for countless decades to maintain a constancy of purpose. Those who criticize the bars as poor places to meet people miss the point of their place in gay survival.

Greg has always been one in a bar to stand back and watch, sometimes for a few hours at a time, the ebb and flow of people making or renewing a community of their own again and again each night. As in any community, some are left out on the periphery. Some receive far more attention than they perhaps warrant, for such is the nature of charisma. Some have it, and others never will. To criticize that is to complain about animals with a certain commanding scent, or strength of presence, that allows them to lead a herd on thousand-mile journeys in a wilderness.

Even if beauty isn't always truth and truth not always beauty in the gay community, people employ the tools and gifts they're given. More power to the ones who succeed. Greg only finds fault with those who waste their talents shamefully by flying from affair to affair, making a shambles of the lives of those in their wake, without thought to consequences or any sense of remorse. Not because they should but because they *can* break other hearts do they often continue to go forth and conquer. In the play *Our Town*, Thornton Wilder has the Stage Manager say, "'People are meant to live two-by-two.'" He did not, of course, mean two-by-two-by-two-by-two, off into infinity like the mirror images in *Garbo's*.

In a candy store, just because one *can* sample all of the wares does not mean that one *should* or should even try. Enough, however, of lecturing, Greg chides himself.

He spends his first few minutes delving into the minds of others, to set about matching them off, like Dolly Levi. Sometimes, one is as equally interested in the other, yet each is sending up smoke signals as if in a strong wind. The message easily gets lost and the two go off once more, separately. A compatible few tonight he introduces; then he walks off, leaving them to their own devices.

"Is he a friend of yours?" one asks, grateful for the opportunity.

"No," the other smiles, puzzled. "I thought he was a friend of *yours*."

They pass it off since anyone in a small enough community like Denver can learn the names of others and introduce them. Still....

Greg notices one man sitting by himself, just enough away from the others, appearing ever so slightly preoccupied, even troubled. Greg guesses mid-30s. His haircut and the way he dresses, the way he holds himself, denotes military, possibly. Greg doesn't need to read minds; this comes from years of observing others in bars all over the country. Something about his handsome features looks ever the slightest bit familiar. Where was it? More importantly, when was it? Maybe he isn't even someone Greg used to know. Curiosity gets the better of him.

"I saw you sitting by yourself over here, so I thought I'd introduce myself. I'm Greg."

"Oh, hi," the other remarks, just a bit nervously, in a way that comes across as charming. "I'm Paul."

He offers his hand and Greg firmly shakes it.

"I guess I have been looking at you now and then across the way," Paul admits.

"I wasn't sure," Greg smiles, confidently. "But I thought I'd take a chance that you might be interested in meeting. May I take a seat?"

"Of course," Paul grins, scooting his chair over and pulling up another white molded-plastic one for Greg.

"Are you in the service?" Greg asks directly.

"Uh, yeah, I am," confesses Paul. "Does it show?"

"Only to me," Greg says, warmly. "I was in the Air Force."

"*I'm* in the Air Force," Paul tells him, pleased that they have something in common. "Where were you stationed?"

"My last assignment was the Air Force Academy."

"Really? When? I was a cadet there in the mid-'80's."

123

"I resigned in 1979," Greg admits, knowing that Paul could not have been one of the cadets who were there when he taught.

"Oh, I see," Paul says, disappointed. "I thought I might have known you then. But I guess not. I graduated in 1988."

"I thought that you looked familiar, too. So you started in 1984?"

"Yes."

"What did you major in?"

"I was a Humanities major."

"You didn't have a pilot assignment?"

"No. I went into missiles."

"Are you originally from Texas?" Greg asks, finding the link if Paul will only confirm. It can't really be possible, though.

"Yes," Paul nods. "How did you know?"

"On Labor Day, 1985, just before your sophomore year, you rode up the Cog Railway to the top of Pike's Peak with your father and sister."

"I did," Paul recalls, surprised. "I remember that day as if it were yesterday. How did you know that?"

"On the way back down the mountain, you sat next to, and struck up a conversation with, an older guy who used to teach at the Academy and who knew that the acronym 'SCUBA' stood for 'Self-contained Underwater Breathing Apparatus.'"

"Oh, my. That was you?"

"Yes, Paul," Greg sighs, immensely relieved. "That was I. Long ago, I gave up thinking that I'd ever see you again."

Chapter Forty

"I was hoping you were going to give me your phone number that day before my family and I drove off," Paul soon confesses.

"I wanted to, but I didn't have any business cards to give you and no pen on me to write with. Besides, I wasn't sure that you were interested," Greg tells him, his voice touched with regret.

"Didn't I *act* interested?" Paul says. "Good grief. We talked the entire way down the mountain. I virtually ignored my dad and sister the whole time."

"I know, but I thought that maybe you were straight," Greg says, disappointed at all the years that they've wasted.

"Well, I'm not straight," Paul chuckles, with a touch of sadness in his voice. "Of course, I couldn't come out and tell you that I was gay on the train, could I?"

"No."

"When you didn't offer to give me your phone number, I assumed that the guy you were with was your lover," Paul explains.

"Dino? No," Greg tells him, emphatically. "We were friends. We still are friends."

"I didn't know your last name; and besides, I also thought you weren't interested."

"I was very interested," Greg reveals. "And for years after, I kicked myself for not coming up with some way to give you my phone number. A few years later, when I told my friend Roger about the incident, he asked, 'Why didn't you just tell him your last name and that you were in the phone book?'"

"He was right," Paul states, pointedly. "You could have. I would have looked up your number and called."

"I was brain-dead that day. And to think that maybe we could have been together all these years?" Greg states, sadly.

"That was a distinct possibility since each of us obviously found the other attractive and interesting," Paul smiles.

"Have you had a partner?" Greg asks.

"Not really. It's difficult in the service, as you know," Paul confesses. "And you?"

"No," Greg says, shaking his head. "Not really."

"We could always start over, you know," Paul ventures. "I still think that you're quite handsome and interesting to be around."

"All these years later?"

"Yes, all these years later. We have a lot of catching up to do, though."

"That's fine with me. But when I saw you earlier, I got a sense that something is troubling you. Am I right?"

"You had to remind me," Paul says, looking down. "I keep trying to forget, but I can't. I've gotten involved in something that I must prevent from happening, but I don't know how."

"You can tell me about it," Greg offers. "Maybe I can help?"

"No," Paul says, shaking his head emphatically. "No one can help with this. It's too bizarre."

"I don't know. Try me. You might find that I can be far more helpful than you think."

"I don't see how."

"Trust me."

Paul reluctantly relates a story that even Greg finds unbelievable. Yet he senses that Paul is telling him the truth. It seems that the Wing Commander at the missile base where Paul is stationed has been methodically and carefully recruiting other officers into a diabolical and absurd plot to launch a few intercontinental ballistic missiles against former Republics of the USSR.

Paul explains why, "They don't like what has happened to the professional military might of America lately, ever since the old USSR military empire broke apart. They resent that budgets have been cut, officer slots eliminated, strategic ships and aircraft retired. They hope that, after a nuclear attack, the USSR will be reestablished, the Cold War will resume as it used to be, and the U.S. will again fund a massive arms race, as it has so often in the past."

"Oh, brother, he is a lunatic," Greg exhales, worried. "This sounds a little like the plot from that *Star Trek* movie a couple of years ago."

"Who knows?" Paul shrugs. "He could have gotten an idea from that film. He may be a lunatic, but he's quite intelligent."

"Yeah, but in the movie," Greg reminds him, "the bad guys are thwarted, their plot foiled. Besides, that was a movie; this is real life. Doesn't he care that thousands of people might die? That these nuclear detonations will poison the earth, making Chernobyl look like a picnic?"

"He wouldn't care if he thought about it; however, he intends to target uninhabited areas in Russia and the Ukraine. He wants their former military might restored, not crippled, so he intends to infuriate them, not damage their capacity to rebuild."

"Even if the U.S. admits that a few military men on our lunatic fringe have perpetrated this plot, the seeds of suspicion will be re-sown," Greg states. "The Russian people then will no doubt welcome the return of the communists to power. At least under the communists, their economy was managed, and no one dared to attack them after World War II."

"Exactly," Paul confirms. "Colonel Traxall doesn't even have to seek out anyone in the Russian military to support his plans. Although several would probably invite this attack if they knew about it because they'll benefit, too."

"It certainly sounds like some kind of plot out of one of those Clancy novels from the 1980's, doesn't it?" Greg replies.

"Yes, it does. I'm sure many writers of that genre are sorry that their old Cold War nemesis is gone. It's cheated them out of millions in book sales, I'm sure. Like James Bond without *Spectre* or *Thrush.*"

"So how did Traxall involve you?" Greg asks, coming to the main point.

"He found out somehow that I was gay and threatened to expose me," Paul admits.

"Ah, the old justification for excluding gays from the military: we're easy targets for blackmail," Greg sighs, but he looks at Paul directly and asks, "But why should you care?"

"I don't!" Paul exclaims. "Even if my family didn't already know, I still wouldn't have gone along with this, but I've pretended that it mattered to me, to see if I could somehow stop them."

"But you haven't found any way?"

"No," Paul admits. "I don't even know who is involved or how many other officers have been recruited. He hasn't even told me how he intends to pull it off. Somehow, I thought he'd be a little less secretive."

"He sounds clever, to say the least," Greg agrees. "This way, nobody involved knows the entire plot but him."

"And if I went to the OSI now," Paul explains, "they'd simply think I was crazy."

"And they'd kick you out for being a lunatic or being gay," Greg nods. "Either way, you're out of the picture and Traxall succeeds with his plot using others."

"Now are you sure that you want to get involved?" Paul asks him directly.

"More than ever," Greg tells him. "By the way, why have you come to Denver?"

"I already had leave scheduled," Paul says. "But I just wanted to get away from the air base and Traxall, to think things through. I'm not exactly sure why I picked Denver, but I haven't been here in several years. I guess I was trying to recapture the old days when I used to come up here from the Academy. It's certainly a strange coincidence meeting you again after all this time."

"I don't believe in coincidences," Greg smiles.

"What do you mean?"

Greg takes a deep breath, and then begins, "Since you've told me quite a story and I've believed you, you're going to have to suspend disbelief while I tell you *my* story. I have a sneaking suspicion that perhaps our two stories have more in common than either of us knows."

Not only does Greg tell him the details of the past several days, he plants selected images in Paul's mind of the important stages, as they occurred. By the conclusion, Paul is amazed.

"That is utterly fantastic," he responds. "And I believe every word of it. I could see and feel everything that you experienced, as if I were there. And you say that you can read minds too?"

"Yes," Greg confirms.

128

"Then you could read Traxall's mind? Find out all about his plot and who is involved?" Paul gasps.

"Yes, I could," confirms Greg.

"I almost can't believe it's possible. I've been wrestling with this dilemma for weeks, wondering what to do. This is like a miracle, meeting you here," Paul confesses.

"I would agree," Greg grins. "So where are you staying, now that you're in Denver?"

"I just arrived today," Paul explains. "I was planning to check into a hotel tonight."

"Well, obviously," Greg offers, "you'll stay at my place. You can have my bed and I'll take the couch."

"I'm sure there's room enough in your bed for two," Paul ventures.

"Now who's the mind reader?" Greg laughs.

Chapter Forty-one

In the morning, it doesn't take a telepath to know when two people who are together seem intended for each other. Even Sneezer and Schnozz take to Paul immediately, filling up the bed with their furry presence and decisive approval. They make a most contented foursome.

Both Paul and Greg awaken at approximately the same time, kissing long and passionately, each in the other's arms as if nature had designed a perfect fit of one form to the other.

"I'm glad you like cats," Greg says, smiling and running his hand along Paul's firm arm.

"I love cats," Paul exclaims, grabbing Sneezer and hugging him. "You can't really keep cats as easily in the military. I was still planning to get one, though. These two are wonderful."

"They've taken to you more than I've ever seen before. I'm glad," Greg beams.

"Are you sure that you didn't work a little of your magic on them so that they'd like me?" Paul inquires, slyly.

"Not a bit," Greg insists. "They're just good at judging character."

"And to think that you won the lottery and gained these amazing abilities at the same time. I'm impressed."

"It doesn't bother you," Greg asks, still concerned, "that I can read minds and do all these other things?"

"Of course not," Paul admits. "You promised not to use your powers on me if I didn't want you to, and I trust you. You obviously had the courage to tell me even though you said it might bother me. I'm flattered that you've trusted me."

"You should be. Nine years ago, I thought you were wonderful and handsome. I feel even more strongly now."

"Thanks," Paul confirms. Then his tone grows more serious, "Besides, you're willing to risk your life to stop this megalomaniac and get me out of this terrible predicament. I'd be a fool not to be attracted to you again. You're even more handsome with that gray hair."

"Don't stop. I love flattery," Greg laughs.

"No more. You'll get a swell head," Paul smiles, holding Greg's head in his lap. "What do you have in the way of food for breakfast? I'm starving, and I'm even more wonderful in the kitchen."

"Than you are in bed?" Greg laughs. "That hardly seems possible."

"Hey, some girls got it and others don't," Paul grins, checking his nails.

"There's plenty of food for breakfast," Greg confirms.

"Then let's get our butts out of bed and take a shower. We're both sticky."

"And sweaty!" Greg adds. "But you should know that Denver has a water shortage."

"So, we'll shower together," Paul determines.

"Great!" Greg readily agrees. "It's an environmentally sound decision."

"As long as we don't stay in there forever," Paul admonishes, casting a sneaky look at Greg.

"I promise. In and out," Greg insists.

"That's what you told me last night," Paul laughs, pushing Greg off his lap and out of bed.

Much later, Greg enters the kitchen, drying his hair with a towel just in time to catch Paul slipping Schnozz some bacon, her favorite human food.

"Ah, ha!" Greg announces. "You've discovered that the way to this man's heart is through his cat's stomach." He reaches out and pulls Paul close, kissing him again.

"Hey, I'm no fool," Paul admits. "Besides, I've cooked plenty. I don't know how much you superheroes eat for breakfast."

"Superhero is a bit much, don't you think?" Greg smiles, although he likes the sound of it, coming from Paul.

"I'm surprised that you haven't made yourself one of those superhero costumes, the kind with a long, flowing cape," Paul teases.

"Aw, I'm lousy with a needle and thread. Besides, I think I'd look silly in tights, with a big 'G' stenciled on my chest."

"On the contrary," Paul confesses, rubbing Greg's muscular pectorals, "I think you'd look stunning in any formfitting clothing. You look fabulous naked."

"You're not so bad yourself," Greg replies, messaging Paul's back.

"We better quit while the food is still warm," Paul warns.

"I guess you're right. Besides, I have to call work and tell them that I will be taking the next two weeks off."

"Won't they mind?"

"Fortunately, this month the announcement schedule is light. I'm sure they won't object to my taking time off to save the world as we know it."

"Good. I want to spend more time with you before we have to get back to North Dakota next weekend when my leave is up," Paul advises.

"That will give us plenty of time to think about how we're going to dispatch Traxall and his evil minions."

"I wish we could just will the whole thing away," Paul sighs.

"Maybe we can. Willing it away is part of what I had planned."

Chapter Forty-two

The next few days for Greg and Paul are idyllic as they become personally and intimately acquainted. Riding bikes along Denver's many urban bike trails, visiting museums and the Denver Botanic Gardens east of Cheesman Park, attending an IMAX show in City Park, or simply buying groceries at "Queen" Soopers and preparing meals together as they discover intensities of shared emotions and commonalities that they had hoped, but dared not expect, to find so readily. They initiate the never-ending process whereby two individuals become a couple and move onward from there. Each has known years of establishing separate identities so that now, both fervently desire, these new efforts will forge them as one.

At every opportunity, however, Greg cannot neglect his telepathic networking. The many civic projects that he began the previous week still take up much of his time as he revisits the former gang-infested neighborhoods, the streets and bridges where the homeless live, and even the middle class and affluent regions where deep troubles can develop if not looked after. This is a new era, when a man's home is no longer his castle; and he is certainly not the ultimate lord of the manor, bending all others to his will. These times require shared responsibilities, and several homes have no man in the former sense. Yet this is also an evolving time, when privacy must balance with community, so that the hushed abuses of former years are no longer allowed to fester in conspiracies of silence and malignant neglect. Greg knows that he must equally aid those who weep silently as well as those who cry out loud for help. Either he must answer their cries, or he directs others to uncover the problems that he has overheard. Often, many answers can be found within when the right questions are asked.

At each turn in the road or trail, Paul is by him, amazed at the dedication, the caring, and the concern of this man whom he only now begins to know and understand. He is, indeed, an ordinary man with extraordinary powers; but he does not allow himself to remain the sole arbiter, the one with all of the right answers. Always questioning, forever adjusting, but acting firmly when the need arises, he responds to so many needs. Paul sees that the short-term solutions are usually the easiest. Long-term answers, Greg tells him, are those that others must work toward.

"I facilitate," Greg explains to him at one point.

Asked what he means, he delineates: "When I first worked at BMI, I took the minutes of meetings in which a facilitator controlled the flow of discussion regarding each group we interviewed and documented. BMI was attempting to streamline their entire import and export business. Consequently, all groups had to attend these sessions, explain what it is that they did, and from within each business group, from within themselves and their own resources, with the facilitator's help, discover the best solutions for improvement."

"I see," replies Paul, becoming more impressed that Greg has been groomed, historically, for this current mission that he's been on.

Remembering his courses at the Academy, he recalls Abraham Lincoln, whom no one else could have replaced, successfully, as president of the United States during the Civil War. No other man had the talent, the quiet and firm tenacity, and especially the almost sacred temperament to endure fatiguing senators, a disturbed wife, tiresome and greedy business leaders, ineffectual and failing generals, a determined and ferocious foe, a wavering electorate, an often hostile and vicious press, and an endlessly grim and painfully debilitating war. And he succeeded where virtually no one else at the time would have. Oh, he had help; but because he won the war, looking back, anyone might be forgiven for considering the outcome inevitable. It was not. Take a brick or two out of the wall, a chemical or component out of the mix, and the United States might have become, possibly even to this day, disunited. What a terrible consequence that would have been for the world in later years, one can only speculate at length and uselessly.

Matching the right man to the times, Paul realizes, watching Greg leaving sandwiches for the poor under a bridge, is a dicey thing. An Alexander can build an empire, an Abraham Lincoln win a war, but the peace that follows can entirely come undone in the hands of lesser men. Still, the world as they changed it feels an imprint, as

134

permanent as men's and women's footsteps can be. Some men and women, certainly, step off in bigger shoes.

Chapter Forty-three

"Pull over here," Greg tells Paul, who is driving south on Corona Street, just north of 11th.

The two of them have been to one of the big electronics stores on Colorado Boulevard, near I-25. Without explanation, Greg purchased a modest Sony CD boom box and three Barbra Striesand CDs. He also has the latest issue of *Out* magazine tucked under his arm.

Paul looks up as he eases into a parking spot on the street and sees a pale blue and white sign: "Project Angel Heart."

"Do you want to come in with me?" Greg asks.

"Sure." Paul has quickly learned that any place Greg visits usually becomes some kind of surprise or adventure not to be missed.

They walk up the steps, through the front door, and stop at the receptionist's desk, "Hi, Betty. Is Bob still in room Four?"

"Yes," she smiles, cheerfully. "I'm sure he'll be glad to see you again. Your visits always seem to perk him up."

"I'm glad," Greg says, breezing past her desk and down the hallway, Paul following in his wake with the boom box and the CDs.

Entering the room, Greg calls out to a man lying in a bed, "Hey, buddy, I brought you some music by 'Babs' as I promised. I also brought my new boyfriend, Paul."

Greg turns to Paul, "Bob says 'hi' and asks how you're doing?"

"Uh, fine," Paul mumbles, confused, looking back and forth at Greg and Bob, who hasn't said a word from the bed. Bob's eyes have that look of a light bulb with its filaments burned out.

Greg explains, "Bob can't speak and can't see, but he can hear fine and his mind's alert." Greg sits down in a chair next to the bed and holds Bob's hand firmly.

"Yes, I brought the latest issue of *Out* with me. It's got some good articles."

For the next several minutes, Greg and Paul take turns reading some of the more interesting pieces to Bob, especially the movie and book reviews. Whenever Bob has questions or comments, Greg reads his thoughts and passes them along to Paul.

At one point, Greg says aloud, "Yes, he is. More handsome than I deserve. Yeah, I think I do."

"What did he ask?" Paul questions, setting down the magazine.

"He wanted to know if you're attractive," Greg smiles.

Paul leans over and kisses Greg softly on the cheek, "Thanks."

"And then he asked me if I love you."

Paul's face fills with affection. He stands up, moves behind Greg, reaching his arms around Greg's strong shoulders, and hugs him tightly. "Bob," Paul says firmly, "I love Greg."

Before they must leave, Greg sets up the boom box and slips in one of the CDs. A tear comes to Bob's vacant eyes as his favorite pop diva begins to sing, "Memories light the corners of my mind...."

Greg gives Bob a massive good-bye hug; Paul does the same, a tear forming as he lays the debilitated man gently down on the bed.

"Call me if you need anything, OK?" Greg tells him from the doorway.

He stops at the front desk and tells Betty, "In about an hour, you might want to put on a different CD for him. I left them on the nightstand."

She gets up and hugs Greg, "Thanks for coming."

"My pleasure. You have a good day."

"Thank you. Bye," she waves as they head down the front steps.

In the car, Paul asks, "How did you learn about him?"

"A few days ago, I was on my way into Category Six Books around the corner when I heard his mind calling out. I simply answered him and we struck up a conversation. He told me that Barbra Striesand is his favorite singer; but in his condition, he couldn't easily tell the staff that he wanted to hear her sing."

"You told him to call you," Paul remembers hearing. "How can he do that?"

"My apartment is only a few blocks away. I've trained my mind to hear his mind trying to contact me. It's faint, but he can be

137

very persistent. If he needs something, I call up the staff and let them know."

"Don't they get suspicious?"

"When you deal with AIDS and its victims as they do all of the time, you learn not to question the few miracles that happen to come along."

Chapter Forty-four

Unfortunately, the day soon arrives when Paul must return to Minot Air Force Base, north of Minot, North Dakota, the missile base where Greg was stationed in the mid-'70's.

Even though there is much that Greg can still do in Denver, he has to accompany Paul and try to stop Colonel Traxall. Sadly, that effort right now has more of a priority than helping the poor and needy people of The Mile High City.

"Madmen too often demand history's constant attention," Greg says, wistfully, as he helps pack Paul's Blazer for their drive north.

"You don't have to go, you know," Paul says, fearful of what awaits them.

Greg looks at him hard, "You know that I have to go. This is probably why I have been given these powers. Surely you've suspected that just as I have. It cannot be mere coincidence."

"I know," Paul tells him, shaking his head. "I just don't want anything to happen to you."

"Nor I, you," Greg responds. "But I don't intend to send you on your way alone, and then look up and see several nukes hurtling overhead, bound for Russia."

"Uh, Greg," Paul carefully reminds him, "they're programmed to fly north, over the Pole, to hit Russia. Not south over Denver."

"Just seeing if you're paying attention," Greg grins. "Anyway, sometimes we have to sacrifice ourselves for the greater good. I know that now."

"What do you mean?"

"Just these past few days, I finally realized that maybe the crazy cadet who ruined my career was the actual target of fate and not me."

"I'm not sure that I follow you."

"Instead of his knocking *my* career off course, perhaps I was there to divert *him* from a military career," Greg surmises. "For

139

years, I thought only in terms of how *I* was affected, how badly *I* felt. But I did assist in ridding the Academy of a cadet who might have become another Colonel Traxall, even if it did cost me my own career."

"He was forced to resign for lying during the investigation, wasn't he?"

"Yes," Greg confirms. "How badly might he have damaged the Air Force had he been able to graduate from the Academy and get out into the real military world in some critical assignment? If he betrayed me, someone who cared very much for him, how might he have betrayed the Air Force or the country? The damage might have been inestimable."

"And your sacrifice, then, unintended perhaps, undid him?"

"Right," Greg accepts, sadly. "Sometimes, a visible target is necessary to expose an invisible one."

"I see what you mean."

"Well," Greg declares, "enough rummaging through the past. It's over. We better get moving."

"So, Ramsey will take care of the cats while we're gone?"

"Yes. He has a key."

In the apartment, both Greg and Paul pick up each cat and give it a long hug, unsure if either will make it back. Greg hugs Schnozz particularly tightly for they have been together for so many years. Schnozz looks at him, puzzled, then reaches over with her paw and pulls his face toward hers. Tenderly, she licks his chin.

"Thanks, Schnozz," Greg softly says to her. "You be good now and don't pick on Sneezer too much. And please don't pee on the bed while I'm gone just because Ramsey's a little late feeding you."

Paul laughs in spite of how he feels as he watches Greg lovingly set her down on the carpet.

From the doorway, Greg waves at the two of them, who sit stoically, side by side, while blankly looking up at him. Then he pulls the door closed behind him and locks it.

Chapter Forty-five

The drive northward allows the two of them to plot possible strategies and to compare their mutual experiences in missile operations as Deputies (DMCCC) and then as Missile Combat Crew Commanders (MCCC), working at one of the 15 separate Launch Control Centers (LCCs) that are buried as much as 60 feet under the soil of North Dakota.

"When were you stationed in Minot?" Paul asks.

"From January 1974 until June of 1978, before I got the Academy assignment," Greg details. "Longest four years of my life."

"How many alerts did you pull?"

"I tried to figure it out once and came up with at least 235 alerts," Greg tells him, shaking his head. "The first half was under the old 36-hour alert system instead of the later 24-hour alerts."

"That's what the crew bunk rooms upstairs were for, then, the 36-hour alerts?"

"Yep. You'd be downstairs for 12 hours, and then sleep upstairs for another 12 hours while the second crew was on alert. Eventually, you'd replace them for the final 12 hours while they slept upstairs," Greg explains.

"Then, when they wanted to save money and cut down on the number of required crew members, they came up with that little adhesive strip to put over the enable and launch panels?"

"They still use them, do they?" Greg sighs. "Seems kind of silly, doesn't it? They cut one-third of the crew force by putting a piece of magic tape over the panels to provide evidence of tampering, and then they proclaim that one of the two crew members on duty can now legally sleep."

Greg then confesses, "We always used to sleep, you know, even during 36-hour alerts when both crewmen were supposed to be awake all of the time."

"It's difficult to stay awake at 4 o'clock in the morning, especially on 24-hour alerts when one of you is authorized to sleep," Paul says.

141

"I remember when my commanders, and later my deputies, would be taking the first sleep shift and I'd be awake. At two in the morning, I'd stand back at the toilet, looking into the mirror over the sink, and wonder if I'd ever been anywhere else except down there on alert," Greg admits. "Time passed so slowly."

"Right," Paul confirms. "And then back on base, you could hardly imagine being out on alert. It's like some terrible memory that you aren't quite certain is real."

"How many blizzards have you been out during?" Greg inquires.

"Two. How about you?"

"Three. One of them lasted four days!"

"You were stuck out in the field for four days?" Paul asks, incredulous.

"Yes," Greg nods. "It was 1975, I think, in January. The winds blew and the snows came down for four consecutive days. People were stranded everywhere. Nothing moved over most of the state of North Dakota. Friends in the housing area had to crawl through their attics to get to their neighbor's houses to share food even though their duplexes were joined and their front doors were only a few feet apart."

"How cold was it?" Paul asks, smiling at the old joke.

"Minus 100 degrees wind chill!" Greg laughs. "It was unreal. People froze to death if they were stuck in their cars and tried to walk toward lights they saw in the distance. At the site we were running out of food and milk to drink. We started rationing since we weren't certain when we'd be relieved. Eventually, I borrowed a quarter from my commander to buy a soda at the machine upstairs."

"What happened?" Paul wonders, sensing that there is more to this story.

"The damned machine ate it!" Greg sighs. "I stood looking at that big red soda machine from hell for several seconds. I really wanted to beat it to death, but I was too exhausted. I knew that if I didn't go to the crew room to sleep, I'd start crying. I'd craved that soda so much all day long."

"Nothing much has changed in missiles," Paul grins, "except perhaps the price of a soda."

142

"What's it like nowadays, going out on alert?" Greg asks. "Back in the 70's, a few of us still figured that nuclear war with the Soviets was possible, even if unlikely."

"You probably read that our missiles are no longer aimed at predetermined targets, although we can still retarget them in a flash, if necessary."

"Yeah. I read that recently."

"Well, for crew members these days, it's an even more thankless task, going out for seven or eight 24-hour alerts each month. We actually don't have any more nuclear enemies, so that we don't expect to be receiving hits by incoming Soviet missiles like you guys might have. Now, it's more of a joke, especially our training about what to do *after* a nuclear attack."

"Well, you have to remember that the mission of the Strategic Air Command in those days was *deterrence*," Greg reminds him.

"Right. And if you were ever required to perform the job that you were trained for, which was launching missiles, you would have *failed* in your mission," Paul laughs derisively.

"Now, if that wasn't some supreme Orwellian example of doublethink, I don't know what is."

"You're right," Paul nods.

"No wonder," Greg finally concludes, soberly, "someone like Colonel Traxall can function in such an environment without anyone else catching on that he's crazy."

Chapter Forty-six

Reaching the entrance to the air base hours later, Paul pulls up to the guard shack and returns the enlisted man's salute.

"Damn," Greg exclaims, looking around at the golf course on the left, the housing area on the right, as Paul drives on. "This is like getting into some sort of freaky time machine and returning to 1978. I haven't been here since I drove away that June day while listening to Jimmie Rogers singing, 'The World I Used to Know.'"

"It probably hasn't changed that much in the past 17 years; a new building here and there, a few extra coats of government-issue paint," Paul informs him, turning right at the second signal and heading toward the Bachelor Officer Quarters (BOQ) parking lot, just past the Officer's Club.

"This is really where I came of age, so to speak," Greg confides, not feeling it necessary at this point to admit to Paul that he'd had his first two sexual encounters with other men here in the BOQ so many years ago. He does wonder to himself what has happened to Steve and John after all these years since each was engaged to, and soon married, a woman.

Thinking that Greg must be referring to his military career, Paul adds, "Being directly in charge of 10 Minuteman III missiles in a Flight, and indirectly in charge of all 50 missiles in a Squadron, tends to force you to become mature in a hurry."

Greg shifts mental gears and adds, "More firepower with those three Reentry Vehicles (RVs) on each missile than any military commander has ever had in the history of the world; and you can be a crew commander, as I was, as a 1st Lieutenant, 26 years old."

"Imagine what it's like for those officers who are on alert with the big MX Peacekeeper missiles?" Paul interjects.

"Yeah, 10 RVs per missile! If they were ever launched in anger, the world would effectively end."

"Right," Paul concurs. "Then you start to wonder who is crazier: Traxall, or the Pentagon brass who dreamed up these doomsday weapons and scenarios?"

144

"Or all of the presidents and Congresses who provided the funding and the permission to follow through on those programs?" Greg continues.

"And the many civilian companies that designed and built all of the targeting computers, warheads, and delivery systems that make the madness function as advertised?"

"I guess," Greg summarily states, "that Traxall isn't the only co-conspirator, is he?"

"No," Paul replies. "He certainly isn't."

Chapter Forty-seven

After an uneasy night's sleep in Paul's single bed, Greg gets up and goes to the window. He is, once again, preoccupied with the past. It didn't help that Paul has the same room in the BOQ that Greg had, his last year at Minot. The florescent stars that used to be pasted to the bedroom ceiling have long since been painted over, however.

"I think I've had enough coincidences lately," he tells himself as he walks through the living room and into the tiny kitchen in his under shorts, looking for some orange juice in the refrigerator.

"At least they've finally replaced that huge, solid oak furniture that we used to have," Greg smiles. "It could have sustained a direct hit, it was so sturdy."

Ghosts from his past thickly haunt him here, however, as he sits down on the couch to contemplate all the turns in life that brought him here the first time and have now brought him back.

Tom, the Air Defense Command pilot and Academy grad, who was later killed in an F-15 crash in Arizona, used to fly the vintage T-33s here. Greg wrote a poem then about Tom, Larry, and Roger, his good friend, all three of whom flew together for the "Spitten' Kittens," the ADC unit on base.

Tom used to play sincere John Denver songs on his guitar in his BOQ room just around the corner of the hallway here. Blond, attractive, bright, well liked, a natural pilot, Roger used to say. Larry, the muscular, hairy-chested Academy grad whom Greg always lusted after, lived across the hall from Tom. Roger, their ringleader and commander, lived next door, with that huge and ugly tapestry of dogs playing cards, hanging on his wall. The four of them gathered in Roger's room on Sunday mornings and made scrambled eggs with cheese and hot frosted Danish rolls. A cholesterol feast.

What becomes of people after they die, Greg wonders, those who used to be good friends during your good years, your 20's, when so much still seems possible? Will they be on the other side of that rushing tunnel to greet you before you walk with the Being of Light?

146

The Being who reviews with you your life, without assigning guilt or punishment?

What if there is no heaven or hell? Nor even a place where knowledge is valued, where this Being of Light dwells? What if we are informed after we die that this life, this Earth, *was* heaven, and that most of us simply pissed it all away, foolishly. That's it. Move along. Next.

Greg thinks to himself, "I mean, we have a world of so many possibilities here. We can be anyone or anything. Yet so many people squander this sole existence by becoming bigots, murderers, thieves, liars, cheats, terrorists. The worst kinds are those who do these evil deeds in the name of one god or another, one religious belief or another. They're so certain that they have Absolute Truth in their hands and hearts, and in their minds."

"Are you all right?" Paul asks, yawning as he interrupts Greg's thoughts from the doorway to the bedroom while looking incredibly sexy in his BVDs.

"I'm sorry," Greg apologizes, patting the couch next to him. "Come have a seat. I was just thinking crazy thoughts."

Paul curls up beside him, head on Greg's lap, "You're not worried about our chances, are you?"

"No," Greg says, shaking his head. "I was thinking that I'm the luckiest man in the world because I found you again."

"I'm glad. You know how much I love you, too."

"I know. Many of us never get a first chance at true love, let alone a second. I was incredibly fortunate that we met once more. I was also remembering someone I used to know when I was stationed here. Tom. His family was rich, descended from English royalty, actually. Even Roger was in awe of his skills in an aircraft. But when his plane initially malfunctioned on a training mission, he should have immediately returned to base. He didn't. He thought he had corrected the problem and he flew on."

"What happened next?"

"The F-15 experienced further hydraulic troubles and he was forced to bail out. He didn't make it."

"I'm sorry."

147

"The point is that life had favored him all along. Given him every benefit, every skill he needed to cope, and yet he failed when the true test came, when his better judgment should have carried him through."

"Maybe he had grown overconfident?" Paul offers. "He never assumed that he'd ever fail. You said that he had always been favored before, that he'd never failed at anything he ever did because he was so talented and bright."

Greg ponders this suggestion for several moments, finally nodding, "Maybe you're right. We cannot always assume that life is going to go our way. No matter how successful we are, we cannot be foolishly overconfident. I suppose we shouldn't discard prudence, no matter how favored we may appear to be."

Chapter Forty-eight

After the two of them shower and get dressed, they drive to the 91st Strategic Missile Wing headquarters building where Greg hopes to seek out Colonel Traxall, to size up their adversary unawares. Find out what he intends to do and when he intends it.

Paul officially checks back into his Squadron, the 742nd, Greg's old unit that still resides in the basement with the 740th and 741st Squadrons. "Key to Peace" is still its motto; blue its color.

Although Greg notices that the new crew uniforms are a bit snappier than the rumpled ones they used to wear, not much else has changed in the Squadron offices. As the two of them turn the corner in the hallway, toward the stairwell to leave, they unexpectedly encounter Traxall.

"Well, Captain Graham?" the tall, imposing Colonel smoothly asks. "How was your leave?"

"Uh, fine sir," Paul replies, clearly nervous at the sight of him.

Greg nudges Paul, "Colonel Traxall, this is a friend of mine, Greg. Greg, Colonel John Traxall."

"Glad to meet you, Greg," the Colonel tells him, offering his hand and exerting that too-firm grip that some heterosexual men mistake for a sign of manliness.

"Same to you, Colonel," Greg replies, exerting even more pressure, but not enough to hurt the guy. He uses this opportunity to try and read his adversary's thoughts.

Traxall's eyes suddenly and darkly narrow as he stares suspiciously at Greg, the easy smile of a moment ago now immediately gone.

Greg thinks, "It's as if he knows that I'm trying to read his mind. This has never happened before!" He quickly breaks the link.

The earlier smile has now evolved into a smirk as Traxall prepares to depart, "I hope I see you again, Greg, but I must be going."

He stops for a moment down the hall, "Oh, Captain Graham?"

"Yes, Colonel?"

"Please see me in my office in one hour."

"Yes, sir."

After he has gone, Greg pulls Paul into an empty office and shuts the door. "I got nothing."

"What!" Paul nearly yelps.

"Keep your voice down," Greg orders. "I tried to read his thoughts and got nothing. It was like a great barricade had slammed shut. He seemed to *sense* that I was trying to read his thoughts. I don't know which one of us was the more surprised, but he closed his mind to me and I read nothing."

"What are we going to do?"

"You're going to attend that meeting in one hour. Try and remain calm. He may reveal when he intends to initiate his scheme. My presence may force him to speed up his timetable. I'll head out around this base in your Blazer and see what I can pick up. Liddell-Hart, the English military scientist, always advocated the strategy of the indirect approach. If I can't find out what's in Traxall's mind, I'll have to seek out those whom he's recruited to help him in his plot. They may not know much more than you do, but at least we'll know how many other officers we're dealing with."

Chapter Forty-nine

Greg soon discovers through the other officers recruited that the plan Traxall has devised is simple, direct, and cunning. Only four line crewmembers are involved, not counting Traxall himself.

As Wing Commander, Traxall recently verified with the Emergency War Order (EWO) group which three missiles, their targeting altered, now point all three of their RVs at open spaces in three of the former Soviet Republics: Russia, Kazakhstan, and the Ukraine. This troika constitutes, Greg knows from reading the newspapers in recent months, the three largest of the four former Republics that still maintain ICBMs. Fit these three pieces back together into a military alliance, Traxall must reason, and the weapons' juggernaut that was once the Union of Soviet Socialist Republics is effectively recreated, like a Red Phoenix rising from the ashes. Ashes that Traxall hopes to provide by launching just three Minuteman IIIs.

That unfortunate trinity will release enough radioactive poison into the world's bloodstream to foul U.S. relations with the East for uncountable years, turning the world back to the way it was when Greg was stationed at Minot in the 1970's.

That was a time when framed posters used to hang on the walls of the Wing building showing, graphically, and almost homoerotically, the immense and numerous red-colored Soviet rockets, which easily dwarfed the significantly smaller Titan, Minuteman, and Polaris/Poseidon missiles of the U.S. Never, in all his years of observing the gay community, has Greg encountered such obsessive "Size Queens" as he saw among the heterosexual officers of SAC. Talk about penis envy.

To compensate, intelligence officers during several briefings repeatedly cited "superior throw weight" and the "higher yield and accuracy" of smaller U.S. missiles, Greg remembers. As further compensation for perceived inadequacy, the Pentagon then proposed, and was finally allowed to build, the MX Peacekeeper, nearly as large as the biggest Soviet rockets. The program seemed to soothe, at least for the time being, their overriding sense of inferiority.

But during the Reagan years, when money for weapons was no object, flowing out of a cornucopia of taxpayers' pockets, someone also came up with the bizarre Midgetman missile concept. Build many, small, mobile, single-warhead missiles, presumably to counter the increasing numbers of Soviet rockets. Greg always assumed that this scheme was a giant sexual-inadequacy step backward, but he gave up trying to figure out what the Pentagon's phallic fixation with missiles meant.

Clearly, officers like Traxall cannot accept their lesser role in American society and the world's armories. Being number one in a greatly diminished field isn't sufficient compensation if all of your adversaries are relative pygmies, regardless of their ability to shoot down your helicopters and ambush your Humvees.

"The World's Policeman" isn't a very appealing role when you used to be a colossus who grappled all over the globe with another titan over the very fate of the planet's existence. When the world might be obliterated in a nuclear holocaust instead of merely tormented daily by small groups of terrorists who hide in the Earth's shadows by day and rise up by night. Who, at most, might blow up a single city with a portable atomic device. In no way does this bear any resemblance to a Biblical Armageddon.

Chapter Fifty

Back in Paul's BOQ room, he informs Greg, "It's a go in the morning."

"I thought so. The four crew members who are involved in the conspiracy are going out on alert on the same day, tomorrow," Greg confirms. "I found that out in scheduling. You're going to KILO Launch Control Facility with your deputy, and the other crew is then driving on to MIKE LCF."

"Makes sense. Send us out in the same vehicle," Paul nods.

"The redundancy SAC built into the system was to ensure that the missiles get *launched*, especially during an attack. So only two crews are required to turn two sets of keys, each commander and deputy simultaneously," Greg reminds Paul. "He only needs four of you, as long as they're on the same two crews and on alert in the same squadron."

"Right. They built five, electrically interconnected Launch Control Centers (LCCs) in each Squadron for survivability, figuring that Soviet rockets might knock out, at most, three LCCs, and that the remaining two LCCs could still launch all of the Squadron's 50 missiles."

"Unfortunately," Greg says, "it only takes four determined officers in two LCCs to launch; the others cannot stop them."

"The deterrent threat was all aimed at *Soviet* lunatics bent on starting a nuclear war with a 'first strike' on the U.S. Not enough measures were taken, apparently, to deter our own lunatics from launching."

"The Human Reliability Program is supposed to ferret out lunatics from among the launch crews," Greg states.

"Exactly," Paul confirms. "But they didn't think about what to do when the head lunatic is the Wing Commander. What did you learn about the other crew members?"

"Traxall has something on each of them, just as we figured," Greg explains. "The other commander has been cheating on his wife, and Traxall found out about it. The guy's deputy tested positive for drugs, but Traxall has been able to suppress the results, for now, if the guy cooperates. Your deputy tested positive for HIV, which he got, he thinks, from a female prostitute overseas. Traxall threatens to claim that the guy is gay, and we know how straight guys hate to be accused of being fags."

"We know that Traxall will expose me for being gay if I don't cooperate. So he's using blackmail on all of us, for different reasons," Paul concludes.

"So, regardless of the Pentagon's prejudice against gays, everyone in the military is potentially a blackmail target for one reason or another. Maybe we should just kick everyone out?" Greg laughs, ironically.

"Right," Paul agrees. "But we're the ones who are singled out as potentially unpatriotic and willing to sell out our country."

"That's the part that angers me the most," Greg states. "I resent being considered a potential traitor when there are no American gays who have sold out this country. There are plenty of heterosexuals over the years that have, but they're considered safe risks. It's certainly hypocritical!"

"How did Traxall get the four of us crewed together? The Wing Commander usually doesn't have that kind of authority."

"He convinced your Squadron commander that these two crew pairings would make prime candidates for SAC's annual Olympic Arena missile competition at Vandenberg AFB next year."

"That was clever of him."

"Yes," Greg agrees. "He seems to be a master manipulator. He reminds me of Sherlock Holmes's evil genius adversary, Professor Moriarty, who was always several steps ahead of the authorities. Yet unlike Moriarty, Traxall adds insanity to the mix. That may, in fact, be what is preventing me from reading his mind. What makes him able to detect what I'm trying to do."

"How so?"

"I don't know the scientific or medical explanation for it; I'm not even sure that scientists or doctors today could satisfactorily explain it, given our limited knowledge of how the brain functions and how memory works, but Traxall could be some kind of genetic leap ahead for humankind in the development of the mind. Even with

154

a few of the street people I've worked with who showed significant mental or emotional problems, there were clear paths to follow, in their conscious and subconscious minds, even if they sometimes were a bit confusing."

"And Traxall?"

"I couldn't even seem to locate a way in, a place to start. The complexity of his mind was unlike anything I've previously encountered. And mutations in nature are often virulent--which may be the reason for his madness."

"Why don't we just shoot the bastard and be done with him?" Paul complains, frustrated.

"If only it were that simple. We have to catch him and the others in the act of treason. Otherwise, who's going to believe you or me?"

"They'll just say that I'm a fag officer, trying to ruin Traxall just because the Colonel found out that I was gay."

"Or that I'm an ex-officer fag, trying to protect my lover's career," Greg adds.

"How about if you order the other commander to shoot his deputy, and my deputy to shoot Traxall?" Paul offers.

"We're supposed to be the good guys, Paul. We aren't allowed to sink to the level of our enemies. You know that," Greg smiles, knowing that Paul didn't really mean it. "Didn't you read the superhero manual?"

"I was just testing you, Greg," Paul rationalizes.

Chapter Fifty-one

The next morning, Paul and all of the other crewmembers who are going out on alert this day are gathered in the pre-departure room for the daily briefing. As prearranged, Greg has found a convenient room to hide in just down the hallway, to observe the proceedings through Paul's eyes. They both know that, no matter what happens, Paul will not turn his launch key at the designated time. With Greg slipping into the underground Launch Control Center unobserved during changeover, they can easily subdue the deputy after he first turns the enable switch, in preparation for launching the missiles. No matter what the MIKE crew does, without a second launch vote no missiles are going anywhere.

The plan sounded simple enough when they discussed it earlier. Neither is certain, however, if it will be so simple when the time comes.

This plan, however, offers no means to implicate Colonel Traxall in his treason; but they've determined that stopping the three missiles from launching, thus preventing an almost certain return to the old world order, is their primary responsibility.

The Wing Operation's officer calls the assembled crew members to attention, and then he announces, "Ladies and gentlemen, the Wing Commander."

Greg had forgotten that the Minuteman crew force has been integrated with women in recent years. It certainly was not true when he was stationed at Minot. Wives would have objected to their husbands going out on alert for 24 hours with another woman. Of course, if a mixed crew were composed of a lesbian and a gay man, Greg used to surmise, no hanky-panky would occur. It's only when you put male and female heterosexuals together that you can have trouble. Sometimes, they are unable to control their sexual urges in close proximity to one another.

Greg watches Colonel Traxall walk briskly into the meeting room and up to the podium, "Ladies and gentlemen take your seats."

After everyone has resumed sitting, the Colonel begins: "Since I have come aboard as your commander, I have taken steps to keep in touch with the crew force, getting to know more of you personally as well as professionally. Today, I am instituting a new program. Periodically, I'll be accompanying individual crews to the field where I'll spend an entire alert with them."

There are a few, soft, nearly inaudible groans from the crewmembers, for no one wants to have the Wing Commander in the capsule. It would be like having your parents with you on a date. Crewmembers often rig an LCC for "silent running" by cutting off some of the automated alarms and turning down some of the lights. You cannot do that when you are being observed and must follow all rules to the letter.

Greg can sense that Paul has stiffened, realizing what the Colonel may announce this morning, "*Stay calm, Paul. We'll figure out some way to deal with him if he goes out with you.*"

"This morning, I've decided to go to KILO LCC with Captain Paul Graham and his deputy, Lt. Bill Peavey," the Colonel says, looking directly at Paul and smiling in a way that could easily twist into a leer with very little effort.

Paul blanches but tries to smile as if appreciative of the honor, dubious as it actually is. Several of the other crew commanders exhale audibly, relieved that they will not be visited on this alert.

Greg watches Traxall closely and thinks to himself, "It's almost as if he can sense my hiding behind Paul's eyes. But I'm sure I'm just being paranoid."

With the briefing soon concluded, the crewmembers file out. Another captain who knows Paul draws close and sarcastically whispers, "Have a nice alert."

"Thanks."

Colonel Traxall approaches and tells him, "I'll meet you at the Vehicle Barn."

"That's fine, Colonel."

Greg has already slipped out of the Wing Building and onto the crew bus that will take the crew members to the Vehicle Barn where they'll pick up their Air Force blue Chevy Suburbans, the same

157

make of vehicle the crew force has been driving to alert in all kinds of weather for at least two decades.

Years before, each crew got its own vehicle. But since the early 1970's, with fuel conservation a priority, all crews except those driving to LIMA Launch Control Facility, one of the most distant LCFs, must double up.

The 15 LCFs of the 91st Strategic Missile Wing are laid out in a giant horseshoe shape in the northwest corner of North Dakota. The 742nd Strategic Missile Squadron runs along the northern tier of the horseshoe, as well as the state, with OSCAR LCF directly north of Minot Air Force Base, almost to the Canadian border. The five flights of the 741st SMS form the giant "U" of the horseshoe, almost edging the state of Montana to the west. The 740th Squadron forms the lower portion, south of the city of Minot, with ALPHA LCF well to the southeast.

Each of the 150 Minuteman III missiles is housed separately, underground in its own silo, at its own Launch Facility (LF). Each LF and each LCC are no closer to one another than three nautical miles. The electrical connections between them are replicated such that the Soviets would have had great difficulty launching their missiles, from thousands of miles away and coming over the North Pole, and accurately disrupting communications between enough LCCs and LFs to prevent an effective U.S. retaliation. At least that was the theory.

From the mid-'60's, crews have driven the paved and dirt roads of North Dakota virtually every day to go on alert, passing by wheat farms large and small and through several small towns. OSCAR LCF, the closest site, is approximately 30 minutes away. GOLF and HOTEL, the pair the farthest away, require well over an hour to reach, even on dry roads. In winter, driving times usually increase significantly.

Most crewmembers are on a four-year assignment. After that time, some are able to find other assignments out of the missile occupational field. Others, like lost Dutchmen, transfer back and forth from the various missile bases in the Midwest to Vandenberg Air Force Base in California, the missile training facility, or to Offutt

158

Air Force Base, the headquarters of the Strategic Air Command in Nebraska. They never get out of missiles or SAC.

Missile operations duty is neither glamorous nor desirable. Most SAC missile bases like Minot are not located in garden spots of the nation, even though North Dakota prides itself as "The Peace Garden State," a tribute to the Park that straddles the U.S.-Canadian border and commemorates the state of peace that has usually existed between these two northern hemisphere nations. Unhappy outsiders claim that the state tree of North Dakota is the telephone pole, and the state bird is the mosquito.

For crewmembers, marriages have been known to implode after extended months in missiles at bases like Minot. A few suicide attempts have been made under the pressure of pulling continuous alerts. No different than any average American town, missile bases know philandering, as well as child, spousal, and alcohol abuse. Most families, however, feature heroic husbands and wives who stay together despite all of the difficulties that a long missile assignment imposes. Missiles is, in fact, one of those dirty jobs that someone, unfortunately, must do.

Greg's main concern this day is if Colonel Traxall will be able to detect his presence on the long ride out in the crew vehicle. Since the MIKE crew commander will be driving, Greg realizes that he will have to spend the entire drive in the back, with the luggage.

Crewmembers are required to bring their Technical Order (T.O.) manuals out with them on every alert. Carried in a special black leather T.O. bag, these thick, heavy documents contain all of the normal, non-secret, and authorized technical procedures for performing duties and using equipment while on alert. Crewmembers also haul out large, green, canvas crew bags. In them you can find books, magazines, newspapers, games, foods of all types and quantities, and nearly anything else they can think of that is not flammable, unauthorized, or explosive--to keep themselves entertained while on alert.

After Paul leaves the back door open long enough for Greg to climb in unnoticed, the five visible (and one disguised) occupants head out the main gate and turn north.

159

"I should have ridden on the roof," Greg soon laments to himself, buffeted with every turn. "It would have been more comfortable than projecting an image that I'm a piece of luggage."

Chapter Fifty-two

Nearly an hour later, the MIKE commander stops the vehicle at the high, barbed-wire-topped gate of KILO Launch Control Facility after driving down the lengthy access road. Paul and his deputy grab their black T.O. and green crew bags from the back, but only after Paul has gotten there first to let Greg jump out without being observed. He has found it difficult to entirely maintain a cloak while exerting more than a moderate amount of physical effort. This handicap reminds him of his days at Marine OCS when the Platoon commander complained, "Can't you walk and chew gum at the same time?"

He rarely could.

Colonel Traxall has already walked to the gate and now contacts the security personnel on the gate phone to gain admittance. When permission is granted, the deputy slides the heavy gate along its rollers and the three of them enter the grounds, with Greg still cloaked and following closely behind.

The Flight Security Controller (FSC) in the security center verifies their military IDs and allows them to proceed through the security door to the elevator. The FSC and his four Flight Security Policemen topside are the eyes and ears of the missile combat crew while they are on alert deep underground.

Sitting at his desk after the missile crew and Traxall have walked through the security door, the FSC looks up in time to notice that the door hesitates momentarily before shutting. "Got to get that fixed," he says to himself.

At the elevator, Paul pulls the mesh gate open and holds it there, taking his time loading his two bags onto the elevator after the deputy and Traxall have gotten on.

"*I'm on,*" Greg informs him, telepathically.

As the elevator starts its long descent, they discover that Colonel Traxall is a pacer on an elevator. Perhaps he's a bit claustrophobic, but he begins walking back and forth. Greg has to keep moving to avoid bumping into Traxall, the luggage on the floor, or the deputy. Finally, he slips behind Paul and against the wall so that he won't accidentally be discovered.

The elevator stops and Paul pulls open the gate at the bottom so that all of them can exit at the tunnel junction blast door. The deputy, the workhorse of a missile crew, slowly turns the handle of the massive, heavy, steel, tunnel junction blast door to retract the large, metal pins that fix the door in place in case of an attack. A direct hit by a nuclear warhead would pulverize everything, even 60 feet underground; but the force generated by a warhead that doesn't detonate too closely might be mitigated by the blast door.

Colonel Traxall waits in the tunnel junction between the Launch Control Center (LCC) on the right and the Launch Control Equipment Building (LCEB) on the left, a large room containing support equipment, especially the air conditioning equipment, used during daily operations. During a nuclear attack, the LCC can be totally isolated from the more vulnerable LCEB by shutting vents and using emergency air conditioning and backup power equipment in the LCC.

The deputy closes the tunnel junction blast door, securing the blast pins, and then rejoins his commander who is inspecting equipment in the LCEB.

After their mandatory inspections, they meet again with Colonel Traxall in the tunnel junction. Paul contacts the crew in the LCC over a phone in the tunnel junction to let them know that they are prepared to enter the LCC for crew changeover.

In a few moments, the LCC blast door, a much smaller version of the tunnel junction blast door, slowly opens and Paul, Colonel Traxall, and the deputy bend over and walk through the short, low tunnel that leads to the acoustical enclosure where the on-duty crew commander awaits them as his deputy slowly closes the LCC blast door. Closing either heavy blast door too quickly will cause it to bounce and recoil, a significant mistake for anyone being observed.

The LCC itself is comprised of a thick, outer, cement cocoon that surrounds the acoustical enclosure, a long, large rectangular box that contains most of the targeting computers and communication equipment for the missile combat crew to launch missiles and keep in touch with the topside world and the other LCCs in the Squadron.

162

The enclosure is suspended from the cement capsule by four giant shock absorbers that run through four holes in the ceiling of the acoustical enclosure and attach to the floor. Because of this support system, the entire enclosure can sway a short distance from side to side or front to back if the ground around the LCC trembles.

A short, hinged metal bridge connects the low access tunnel with the acoustical enclosure.

Since Colonel Traxall is present, the on-duty crew follows all procedures by the book. A changeover that might have taken 10 minutes stretches out to nearly 30 minutes as the crew explains the status of KILO flight's 10 missiles and other significant status involving other missiles in the Squadron. Unfortunately, all three missiles that Traxall intends for them to launch are fully operational.

Paul, his deputy, and the other crew are somewhat nervous with the Colonel present, Paul and his deputy having a greater reason to be. However, Traxall is entirely calm, like the guy who gives you your first driving test while you're sweating profusely.

Finally, the changeover completed, the other commander and deputy hand over to Paul and his deputy their side arms, .38 revolvers in black leather holsters, six bullets to a gun, just like the old West. They immediately head for the LCC blast door, with Paul's deputy preceding them and reopening the door. Without looking back, they dash for the tunnel junction blast door, glad for the opportunity to be out of the presence of the Wing Commander.

Paul's deputy closes the LCC blast door, backs out of the access tunnel, and returns across the metal bridge to the acoustical enclosure where Paul, Colonel Traxall, and all of the humming equipment are patiently waiting.

Chapter Fifty-three

Just inside the acoustical enclosure to the right are a toilet and sink, to the left, an emergency air conditioning unit, a refrigerator, and a military cot. All the amenities of home for the nuclear family.

Farther along on the right of the enclosure are also racks of communications equipment, the deputy's console with a TV suspended above it, more communications equipment, and targeting computers. On either side of the enclosure at the far end are two of the four giant shock absorbers. In between them, and just recessed, is the large console for the commander. In the upper portion of the console is the Missile Status Indicator Panel (MSIP) where he can observe the status of the 10 missiles in his flight or switch to display the status of any other flight's 10 missiles. Rows of colored lights, indicating maintenance, operations, launch, and security, show at a glance the status of each missile. The launch panel for the commander is to his right. A 24-hour clock hangs above the console for all to easily observe. The deputy's launch panel is to the left of his console. The enable panel with its thick plastic protective cover, hinged at the bottom, is to the deputy's right. The strips of adhesive tape, that indicate tampering when torn, attach between the plastic cover and the metal panel itself. These must be completely broken to drop the plastic cover and gain access to the enable switch.

As the deputy passes the Colonel, who is sitting on the bed, along the left wall and directly opposite the deputy's console, Traxall reaches up and pulls the deputy's weapon out of its holster, telling him, "You won't be needing this."

"But Colonel," the deputy protests, "we're supposed to be armed whenever anyone else is present in the LCC."

"I'm the Wing Commander, and I'll decide who will be armed. Take a seat," the Colonel orders, his face distorting into a smirk.

The deputy sullenly sits down at his console and slides his chair along its twin rails to the end, just back of the enable panel.

"Oh, Captain Graham?" Traxall smugly sneers, turning to Paul, who is standing in front of his chair at the commander's console at the far end of the LCC, but only a few feet away. "While we're waiting for the MIKE crew to call and tell us that they've arrived, you might as well ask your invisible friend to appear."

"What?" Paul replies, too nervously to fool Traxall. "I don't know what you're talking about."

"Don't fuck with me, Captain," the Colonel threatens, casually fingering the revolver in his hand and then pointing it at Paul. "I've sensed his presence ever since we got here."

Paul hesitates momentarily, hoping that he can bluff the man, "I think you're imagining things, Colonel."

Colonel Traxall pulls back the hammer of the revolver, "There are three of us here to launch these missiles, Captain, not counting your invisible friend. One of us could become superfluous real quick, so he'd better show himself right now."

"All right," a voice calls from the entryway of the enclosure. "Don't pull the trigger. I'll show myself."

The deputy, surprised, swings his chair around and faces the doorway, "Where'd he come from?"

Greg stands visible in the doorway.

Traxall gets up and walks toward the doorway, "Who cares, Lieutenant? But he'll wish that he'd stayed there. I don't like spies interfering with my plans."

The gun in his hand discharges, the bullet striking Greg's kneecap, shattering it. He reaches for the doorway to break his fall but misses and crumples over, pitching sideways over the metal bridge, striking his head against the concrete siding of the capsule and then sliding down into the sewage sump below.

"No!" Paul yells, reaching for his own gun.

Colonel Traxall has already anticipated his move and turned, again pointing the gun at Paul, "Don't even think about using it!"

Paul slowly lifts his hand away from the handle. The deputy, caught in between the two adversaries, and fearing for his own safety, ducks to the floor.

The phone rings, momentarily interrupting this brief standoff.

Traxall steps around the cowering deputy, pushing in the buttons to talk to MIKE LCC with his free hand, while still pointing the gun at Paul. He then picks up the receiver, "This is Colonel Traxall. No, no problems here. Are you ready to enable these birds? Good."

"Deputy!" the Colonel yells at the cringing lieutenant, while keeping an eye on Paul, "Get your cowardly butt up off the floor and over to this enable panel. Then, get ready to turn the switch when I tell you to."

Apparently stunned by the violence, the deputy, standing up, begins to demur, "Uh, sir, you didn't say anyone was going to get hurt. I don't think I can...."

"I told you to *move* lieutenant!"

"No. No, sir!" the deputy responds, shaking but at last emboldened to resist.

Traxall pulls the trigger once again. A stunned look passes over the deputy's face as he clutches his stomach and pitches forward, heavily onto the rails.

Paul again attempts to get his own weapon but Traxall anticipates him, "Too late, Captain. Now, it's just you and me. I *will* shoot you if you don't do exactly as I say."

Traxall raises the phone to his ear once more, "Just a brief delay here, MIKE; but we're ready to enable these birds. Flip your switch."

The Colonel sets the receiver on the console. He first dials the correct launch code into the deputy's launch panel, a code he learned from the Emergency War Order group back on base. He then leans across the deputy's console to flip down the plastic cover over the enable panel, breaking the adhesive strips. He immediately turns the enable switch.

As a look of supreme satisfaction passes across his twisted features, alarms, indicating that two enable votes have successfully gone out to the affected missile launch facilities, sound in all five 742nd LCCs.

He puts the deputy's launch key into the launch panel on the left of the console and picks up the receiver, "MIKE, go ahead and turn your launch keys."

"Now, Captain," Traxall threatens, aiming the gun at Paul's head, "take your launch key, carefully put it into the launch panel, and get ready to turn it on my mark."

Chapter Fifty-four

At LIMA LCC, the commander, napping on the cot, wakes up and asks, still groggy, "What the hell are all those alarms about?"

His deputy, feverishly looking at the printer tape, feeding out profusely, announces, "I don't know sir, but it looks like KILO Ten, MIKE Three, and MIKE Nine have gone enabled!"

Another alarm sounds, and the deputy feeds the printer tape further out, "We've just gotten one launch vote!"

The commander is up off the bed and at his console, staring at the MSIP and flipping the switch to view KILO and then MIKE flights, his worst fears confirmed as enable lights illuminate for the affected LFs.

"Did we get any launch messages from headquarters?" he demands.

"Of course not, Chuck. I'd certainly have awakened you."

"I know. Call the other LCCs and find out what's going on."

The deputy pushes in the buttons, and the comm lines that connect all LCCs are buzzing with panicked conversations.

He soon hangs up, "Only NOVEMBER and OSCAR were on the line, and they claim that they didn't do this. Nobody passed the duress code! None of us could reach MIKE or KILO."

"OK," the commander determines, "call our FSC and have him try to contact the FSCs at KILO and MIKE. Something must be going on at those two sites; otherwise, they'd have been on the lines. I'll try to contact MIKE and KILO over normal telephone lines and see if I can reach them. If we don't reach anyone, we'll have to call a Situation 1 security alert on KILO and MIKE. A fat lot of good that's gonna do if a second launch vote goes out."

"OK, Chuck, I'm calling our FSC."

168

Chapter Fifty-five

Back at KILO LCC, incoming calls are now being ignored, as Traxall confirms on the printer that MIKE has sent its launch vote, "Now, Captain, don't make me have to shoot you, too. Turn your key on my mark!"

Traxall hears a now-familiar voice whisper in his ear, "Three, two, one, Mark! The game's over, Colonel."

Stunned, the Colonel turns to see the deputy standing at his shoulder, evidently quite healthy.

"I shot you dead!" the Colonel insists.

"Wrong, Colonel. Besides, everything is not *quite* as it seems." The deputy's visage disappears and is replaced by Greg's.

"I shot you, too!"

"Also, wrong. Sorry."

Furious, Traxall tries to fire the gun again. It merely clicks. Empty.

"I removed the bullets several minutes ago, before you took the gun from the deputy; or rather, from me, posing as the deputy," Greg explains, wearing one of Paul's crew uniforms to make it easier to disguise himself should anyone catch a glimpse of him this day when he wasn't cloaked or projecting an image other than his own.

"I emptied the gun when I was in the access tunnel after I let the other crew out after changeover," Greg says, turning to Paul. "I got the idea from the Broadway play *Sherlock Holmes* that I saw 20 years ago. There's a scene where Moriarty tricks Holmes out of a gun he's holding; but Holmes, anticipating the evil professor's intent, has surreptitiously removed all of the bullets first."

"All right," Traxall demands, not at all interested, "where's the damned deputy?"

"You'll find him still asleep in the LCEB where I put him into a deep trance before he completed his inspections there. I took his place right after that."

"Nonsense!" Traxall blusters. "I sensed you beside me the entire time I waited in the tunnel junction."

169

"No. I only made you *think* that I was beside you. As a psychic, if you will, a clairvoyant, you're much too susceptible to suggestion, Colonel."

"He's a what?" Paul asks, dumbfounded.

"Not much better than the merest of fortune-tellers or palm readers," Greg laughs derisively. "He has heightened sensitivity and limited psychic awareness, but that is about it."

Angry at being thwarted, the Colonel ignores the insults and remains silent.

"I thought you said that he was an evil genius, perhaps a mentally advanced human being, even if he's insane?"

"Oh, he's crazy, all right," confirms Greg, shaking his head in disgust in the direction of Traxall. "But I misinterpreted his slight psychic prowess for something greater and more elusive. I'd not encountered anyone who has such abilities, even if his are rather mundane. I simply mistook what I sensed for something greater. Chalk it up to my inexperience. I panicked when I realized that he could sense my poking around in his brain. Anyone who knows what I'm up to can block my ability to read his mind, at least temporarily. I didn't realize that before because nobody before Traxall ever knew that I was eavesdropping."

"You're forgiven," Paul tells him, relieved that Traxall's plan has failed.

"OK, damn it," Traxall interjects, "so why did you conjure up all of these charades when you knew that the gun was empty?"

"Come on, Colonel," Greg responds, looking at him in astonishment while wondering how someone who could be so brilliant could also be so dense. "We had to have concrete *proof* of your conspiracy and complicity. Fingerprints had to be on enable panels and launch keys; enable panel covers had to be disturbed and switches had to be turned, with actual enable votes sent, and especially launch keys inserted. Otherwise, nobody would have believed that you were involved when Paul tried to tell them."

Paul adds, "I was never going to insert and turn my key, but we needed to trick you into doing the dirty work, work that you intended the MIKE crew and my crew to do for you. You really didn't trust us, did you?"

170

He gets no response, so he continues: "None of the evidence would have implicated you when we were arrested. But when you announced that you were coming out with us...."

Greg interjects, "...that got the two of us thinking. Why? Then I realized that it wasn't because you thought I'd be along to interfere, or to force Paul and his deputy to do the work. You intended to be here--to shoot them after they launched the missiles."

"Right!" Paul exclaims, indignant. "You were going to use the gun against us and claim that you were only able to wrestle it away *after* the missiles had been launched. You'd claim that you had no idea we were going to launch missiles. You probably hoped that once the MIKE crew realized what had happened to me and my deputy, they'd either commit suicide or die in a hopeless gun battle with the Security Police, trying to break into MIKE LCC."

Greg continues, "You wanted to lessen the odds that any finger of blame would ever point to you by killing off the only other conspirators. That was certainly evil, but smart."

"It would have worked if you hadn't showed up," Colonel Traxall angrily acknowledges.

"You're probably right," Greg agrees. "Even if Paul refused to turn his launch key, you would have been here to kill him, turn the key yourself, shoot the deputy after he turned his key, and then put Paul's fingerprints on his launch key, again hoping that the MIKE crew was gotten out of the way by their own hands or by those of the Security Police. Clever."

"I'm glad that you were here, Greg," Paul says, hugging him.

Traxall indignantly looks away, "Don't make me puke."

Greg just laughs at the homophobe.

Several minutes later, after Paul has called a Situation 1 and transferred his computer-sharing time slot to LIMA, since there is now only one authorized crew member at KILO LCC, they learn that the MIKE crew has surrendered themselves to their Flight Security Controller, transferring their time slot to NOVEMBER.

Greg has planted a detailed visualization in the deputy's mind of how Paul, on his own, thwarted Traxall's scheme.

Unfortunately for Colonel Traxall, as the two Flight Security Policemen haul him topside, he rants about an invisible assistant of

Captain Graham's who played the most important role in stopping him.

"They're both faggots!" the Colonel screams.

When the two Security Policemen look at Paul skeptically, he simply shrugs his shoulders, feigning ignorance. That's enough confirmation for them that their former Wing Commander is certifiably nuts.

Chapter Fifty-six

In response to the situation, two standby crews are dispatched from the base to replace the arrested MIKE crew and Paul's crew, the deputy already on his way back to base, arrested along with Colonel Traxall.

Paul gets off the phone with Wing Headquarters, telling Greg, "They want me to report to the OSI after the relief KILO crew assumes its duty here. I'm to tell them all about Traxall's plot and my involvement in it."

"Nothing will happen to you, will it?" Greg asks, from experience not at all sure whether they should trust the Air Force.

"Oh, no," Paul assures him. "They're just happy that this incident didn't escalate. They are swearing everyone to secrecy on this. Nobody will ever hear about it, not even the President."

"There'll be rumors, you know," Greg asserts.

"Of course, but there are always rumors of one kind or another involving missile duty," Paul reminds him.

"Right," Greg laughs. "I remember when guys up here thought they saw flying saucers hovering over the LFs. Nothing was ever confirmed."

As the two of them sit on the bed together, watching a daytime soap on the TV and waiting for the relief crew to arrive, Greg suddenly gets up, grabs Paul's flashlight, and steps outside the enclosure, pointing the light up at the doorway, remarking, "It's still here."

Getting up, Paul asks, "What's still here?"

"Come take a look."

Paul walks out and glances up at where the beam of light points to a faded strip of newsprint, covered in aged cellophane tape, but still readable, "The best defense against a nuclear weapon is to not be where one goes off."

"That's hilarious," Paul exclaims. "Did you put it there?"

"Yeah," Greg grins. "Twenty years ago. When I was stationed here, I subscribed to the *L.A. Times* newspaper. I used to read the paper on alert. Whenever I came across an amusing statement in an article, I'd cut it out and tape it above the doorway of the LCC where I was on alert that day."

"You mean," inquires Paul, "that there may be more of these?"

"Oh yeah. Over the doorway at LIMA, and over the door to ALPHA, I think."

"But Greg," Paul notices, "it's dark up there. How did you ever expect that anyone would look up and see them? I never have noticed."

"That's the beauty of it, don't you see?" Greg explains. "Years ago, a friend of mine, whose parents owned a motel, was up in a crawl space in the attic, looking for electrical wiring. He got into a very tight spot and noticed something. He looked up and saw a cryptic statement carved into a wooden beam, probably placed there by one of the construction workers when the motel was first built: 'If you're in a position to read this, you're in trouble.' Bill had a wonderful laugh up there by himself, a private little joke left by someone else who had been there before."

"I love it," Paul laughs. "So you deliberately put these phrases in places where only a very few might ever come across them?"

"Right."

"I love you, you silly man," Paul smiles.

"Hey," Greg suggests, gesturing toward the bed, "it'll still be a few more minutes before the relief crew arrives. Let's do something wicked. I never got to when I was stationed here."

Paul rolls his eyes, "I think I know what you've got in mind, and you should be ashamed of yourself."

"Look, straight crew members have probably already done it here, so we won't be the first," Greg replies.

"We don't even have any condoms or lube," Paul insists.

"Actually, we do. I put some in your crew bag this morning while you weren't looking."

"You felt pretty confident about yourself, didn't you?" Paul smiles.

"Actually, I felt pretty confident about both of us."

174

Chapter Fifty-seven

Paul drives the Chevy Suburban brought out by the relief crew. Greg sits on the passenger side, contemplating the many miles, the many years, and the strange transformations that recently brought him back to Minot and to this wonderful man beside him.

"So, how did you figure out that Traxall wasn't as powerful as you first thought?" Paul asks.

"Oh," Greg says, his reverie broken, "I had a long time to think about him while I was riding in the back with the luggage. I figured that if he could sense that I was in the crew vehicle, he would never have allowed me to go along, realizing that I could make myself unnoticeable to others as well as being able to read minds. Then, when he admitted in the LCC that he'd detected my presence only *after* I intended him to, I knew I had overrated his abilities. Besides, why would nature, or Fate, or God give someone who is both evil and insane powers that were greater than those given to me? If evil were ultimately supposed to succeed, then Traxall would have gotten these powers and not me."

"Nevertheless, I'm glad that we succeeded," admits Paul.

"Hey," Greg boasts, "we're the good guys! Why wouldn't we succeed?"

"In world history," Paul reminds him, "good guys don't always win."

"True. But really bad guys eventually fail: The Assyrian Empire. The Mongolian Horde. Hitler and The Third Reich. Soviet Communism in Russia, to name but a few."

"After how many innocent people died?"

"That's the price of vigilance, Paul. If nature is, indeed, neutral, then it is up to humanity to tip the balance on the side of good, against evil and suffering. If we fail to act, we *will* suffer eventually."

After a few miles of silence, Greg asks, "What are you going to tell the OSI?"

175

Paul carefully replies, "I'm going to tell them that I'm gay and that Colonel Traxall tried to use that information to involve me in his plot. He failed. That's an important point to make to them, that we cannot be blackmailed."

"Yes, but you'll be telling them that you're gay. They'll have to discharge you. All of your heroics will be for nothing. None of what you and I did today will ever come out; you've already learned that."

"That's not entirely true," Paul counters. "I met you. Together, we stopped a madman. The Air Force may never admit publicly, but privately they'll know that a gay man saved the world from returning to the old world of Mutually Assured Destruction. Who cares if the world never knows? We know; that's enough for me."

"I see."

"Besides," Paul continues, fondly looking at Greg. "I'm willing to give up my military career to be with you."

Greg turns away, his eyes clouding up as he sees the endless fields of wheat slip past their blue Air Force vehicle. He looks back at Paul and reaches out a firm hand. Paul takes it and holds it as if he'll never let go.

Chapter Fifty-eight

Several weeks later, on a chilly and breezy mountaintop, at a spot sacred to a small group of pagans who worship the blessings of nature and appreciate the power of its elemental forces, the gathered throng awaits the first light of dawn. On hillsides and in mountain meadows below, aspen have already begun their autumnal and inevitable transformation, in anticipation of the latest season of change.

At a given moment, the first ray penetrates the sacred crystal in the hands of the appointed priest and shatters into the many colors of the rainbow. A shaft of this prismatic beam strikes one of the worshipers squarely, enveloping him entirely in a benevolent glow.

"Greg?" the man whispers to his lover beside him, "What does this peculiar tingling mean?"

"Paul," he replies, knowingly, "try to think of it as a gift."

Made in the USA
Middletown, DE
10 March 2022

62459940R00099